"I forbid you to g

She straightened her sh   n
instant he feared she w   speak so
and go anyway.

*Dear God, how have we come to this? Meek Christine defying
me! Please, let us not show ill will before the children.*

He swallowed hard and tried to frame a gentle overture, but
Christine opened her mouth first.

SUSAN PAGE DAVIS and her husband, Jim, have been married thirty-two years and have six children, ages thirteen to thirty. They live in Maine, where they are active in an independent Baptist church. Susan is a homeschooling mother and writes historical romance, mystery, and suspense novels. Visit her Web site at: www.susanpagedavis.com.

Books by Susan Page Davis

HEARTSONG PRESENTS

Don't miss out on any of our super romances. Write to us at the following address for information on our newest releases and club information.

Heartsong Presents Readers' Service
PO Box 721
Uhrichsville, OH 44683

Or visit www.heartsongpresents.com

Abiding Peace

Susan Page Davis

Heartsong Presents

To my aunt, Joyce Page Whitney, and my uncle, Robert Whitney, who are also descendants of blacksmith Richard Otis.

A note from the Author:
I love to hear from my readers! You may correspond with me by writing:

Susan Page Davis
Author Relations
PO Box 721
Uhrichsville, OH 44683

ISBN 978-1-60260-256-4

ABIDING PEACE

Our mission is to publish and distribute inspirational products offering exceptional value and biblical encouragement to the masses.

PRINTED IN THE U.S.A.

one

Cochecho, New Hampshire, 1696

Christine Hardin sat up straight on the backless bench in the meetinghouse as the Reverend Samuel Jewett finished his sermon with a stirring benediction. The congregation rose to blend their voices in the final hymn. Christine glanced sideways, along the line of Jewett children—all five of them, from three-year-old Ruth up to Ben, who was nearly as tall as his father now. At the far end of the row sat the Widow Deane. All eyes stayed forward, except Ruth's. The little girl swiveled her head and looked up at Christine. She smiled and raised her arms in a gesture she used many times a day, begging Christine to pick her up.

Christine couldn't help smiling back at the sweet child, though the reverend wanted his children to be sober in church. She tousled Ruth's dark curls, which were the exact shade of her dead mother's. As she turned toward the pulpit once more, hoping Ruth would follow her example, Christine let her hand rest lightly on the little girl's shoulder. All five of the children grieved their mother, and Christine mourned her dear friend. Each time she looked into the minister's eyes, the emptiness there tore at her heart.

"You may be seated," the Reverend Jewett intoned, and the children stirred and looked to her with confusion. Wasn't it time for dinner?

Christine sat down quickly and pulled Ruth against her side, nodding to Abby and Constance to sit, as well.

The congregation quieted, and the parson raised his voice once more. "Hear ye, hear ye, the marriage banns of Mordecai Wales, a freeman, and Parthenia Jones."

A soft murmur rippled through the congregation.

"A fortnight hence, on the twentieth of August, in the year of our Lord, one thousand, six hundred and ninety-six, the marriage shall take place, if so be the will of the Almighty."

Christine saw ten-year-old John Jewett start to turn his head, but his older brother, Ben, elbowed him. The Jewett family occupied the front pew in church, and the children learned very early that they must never, never look behind them during services. But she recognized how tempting it was just then.

Most of the congregants must be staring at old Farmer Wales. He had buried his second wife a mere month ago, and now it seemed he intended to marry a third—and much younger—woman in two weeks' time. Parthenia Jones was also widowed, and she had two small children. It would no doubt be a good match for her, as Mr. Wales would provide for her and the little ones. She, in return, would take over management of his household and the half-grown offspring of his second marriage. She would tend him in his old age. And, if she didn't succumb in childbirth first, she would be well taken care of after he died.

Still, Parthenia couldn't be more than eight-and-twenty, Christine calculated, and Mordecai Wales must be all of sixty. Ah well, the farmer probably wanted a stout young woman who could work hard and perhaps bear him more children. Christine felt her cheeks redden just for thinking it.

People behind them rose to their feet and shuffled toward the aisle, and she realized the pastor had dismissed them.

On the common outside the stark meetinghouse, Christine's friends, Jane and Sarah, waited for her. Their husbands,

Charles Gardner and Richard Dudley, stood off to one side, talking with Richard's brother Stephen. Charles held his little son, who was eight months old, on one arm, his musket in the other hand. The baby tugged at his father's beard, much to Charles's delight. Ben Jewett, the pastor's eldest son at fourteen, joined the men and was welcomed into the circle.

Christine kept a close hold on Ruth's hand and drew her over to where Jane and Sarah stood. Sarah held her little girl, Hannah, who would soon be a year old. Constance Jewett followed Christine, but Abby flitted off to spend a moment with her friends.

"What did you think of the announcement at the end?" Sarah Dudley asked with arched eyebrows. She shifted Hannah to a more comfortable spot on her hip. Hannah promised to grow up to be as lovely as her mother. Christine was happy that her two friends had found loving husbands who treated them well.

"He didn't waste any time picking out a new wife," Jane noted.

Sarah chuckled. "True. But the marriage will be an improvement in situation for Parthenia, even though he is so much older than she."

"I'm surprised he didn't come courting you, Christine." Jane smiled at her impudently.

Christine shuddered. "Please. You ladies have convinced me by your example that marriage is not necessarily all bad. But to a man of Goodman Wales's years? I think not."

"Aha! You witnessed what she said." Jane turned eagerly to Sarah. "Christine is open to the idea of marriage at last."

"I didn't say that."

"Of course you did," Jane said. "And we must look about for a *young* man for her."

"Or at least one not yet in his dotage." Sarah seemed perfectly willing to enter into Jane's teasing.

"Miss Christine." Constance tugged at her overskirt.

Christine felt a pang of contrition. Here she was gossiping with her friends and setting a poor example for the parson's daughters, who were in her care.

"What is it, Constance?"

"Are you getting married?"

Christine stared down at the six-year-old's innocent face, at a loss for words.

"Not yet," Jane said, reaching out to tweak Constance's braid. "But we shan't stop trying to find a match for her."

"A match?" Constance's brown eyes widened.

"A husband," Sarah said. She glanced at Jane and Christine. "I think this conversation has gone about as far as it should for now."

"I agree. I implore you ladies to put it out of your minds," Christine said. She had long maintained that she had no desire to marry. Indeed, she cringed at the very thought.

Pastor Jewett came out onto the steps of the meetinghouse carrying his musket, which he had traded for in the spring. Renewed threats of Indian attacks had prompted the peace-loving minister to make the purchase. Only two weeks had passed since some of his congregation had been attacked by hostile savages as they left the church service. None of the men went about without their guns these days. He rested it against the wall and spread out a sheet of parchment against the church door, then pulled a hammer from his coat pocket.

"Come, girls. Your father is posting the marriage banns."

"Ah, he'll be wanting his dinner," Jane said.

"Yes. Time to go home." As she turned to look about for Abby and John, Christine noticed a portly woman approaching her. She usually tried to stay out of the path of Mahalia Ackley, who was known for her sharp tongue. Indeed, her reckless gossiping had sent the goodwife to the stocks on more than one occasion. This time there was no avoiding her, however.

"Miss Hardin."

"Good day, ma'am."

The older woman pulled up before her, panting, with her skirts swirling into place. "My hired girl left me last week. Her father moved his family to Cape Cod."

"I heard that." Christine sensed what was coming, but she waited out of courtesy.

"I be looking for a stout girl to do for me. Cleaning and washing mostly, but I hear you're a fair hand with spinning and weaving, too."

Christine forced a smile. She had lived with the Jewett family for nearly a year before the pastor's wife died and still worked for them more than a year after Goody Jewett's death. Her position made her privy to all the secrets of Cochecho, and she knew that Goody Ackley had run through the list of available domestic help in the village.

"I'm sorry I can't accommodate you, ma'am. I've all the work I can handle at the Jewett house."

"Surely the parson's children are old enough to do for themselves."

Christine had the distinct feeling the woman was chiding her. She sought for an appropriate reply. "The children are a big help with the work about the parsonage, to be sure, but the girls are very young yet. They can't do the cooking and washing themselves. Goody Deane and I go across the road nearly every day to help them."

Mahalia Ackley looked furtively about.

Sarah Dudley had joined her in-laws' family and handed Hannah to her husband, but Jane Gardner still stood by Christine, listening with apparent interest.

Goody Ackley took Christine's sleeve between her plump fingers and tugged her aside. She leaned close and said in a confidential tone, "Surely the parson can't pay you much."

Christine felt her cheeks color. She wanted to end this line of conversation firmly, but she couldn't embarrass the pastor by flinging a rude retort at one of his parishioners. She cleared her throat. "I receive adequate compensation, and since Goody Jewett died last year, I feel the family needs me more than ever. You understand."

Goody Ackley's dark eyes snapped with displeasure as she pulled back slightly. "Oh, yes, yes. The poor, motherless children. Some people don't understand that as folks get older they need more help than the able-bodied young ones." She gathered her skirts and whirled away, stirring up dust in the dry churchyard.

Jane stepped closer to Christine. "Good for you. You stayed calm. I'd have spat in her eye."

Christine gave her a rueful smile. "I felt tempted to say what I thought, but. . ."

"I know. It's not in your nature, and it *is* Sunday."

"Their children are all dead or moved away, and I suppose she does need help."

"My husband is waving at me," Jane said. "I suppose we and the Dudleys shall all take dinner at the Heards' today, so the men can discuss building the new pews with Brother William. Of course you mustn't tell the parson they are talking about work on the Sabbath."

Christine chuckled, but Jane seemed to take the matter seriously. She left Christine and joined her husband. The neighbors living close to the meetinghouse opened their homes on Sunday afternoon to the farmers from outside the village, so they would have a place to eat their Sunday dinner in relative comfort. Then all would return to the meetinghouse for the afternoon service, which sometimes went on until the supper hour. Christine waved and gathered the pastor's three little girls about her.

≈

"Goody Deane, be you joining us for dinner at the parsonage today?" Samuel Jewett called to his elderly neighbor, who was saying good-bye to a knot of other ladies.

"Aye, if ye want me," the wrinkled old woman replied.

"Of course we want you."

"Especially if you've baked gingerbread," the impish John added.

Samuel swatted playfully at his younger son. "Here now, be polite. The lady will think you a greedy pig."

"He is that when it comes to gingerbread." Goody Deane cackled as she hobbled along toward the street.

Samuel and Christine matched their steps to hers. John, Ben, and Abby ran ahead, but Ruth toddled along holding her father's hand, and Constance stuck as close to Christine's skirts as a cocklebur.

The two women set to work getting the meal ready as soon as they reached the parsonage. Samuel helped little Ruth change out of her Sunday dress and watched with approval as the children helped carry dishes and set the four pewter plates and mismatched mugs on the table.

He sat down at the table with the two boys and Goody Deane for the first sitting. When they had finished, Christine and Abby quickly washed their dishes and set the table again for themselves, Ruth, and Constance. It was the regular routine of the family. Samuel wished he could afford more dishes, but they got along. Elizabeth had never complained, and he had carved wooden bowls enough to go around. Perhaps he could purchase a couple of tin mugs from the trader. But there were so many other things they needed, and his small stipend was paid only if the tithes amounted to enough to cover it. Members of the congregation occasionally brought his family a load of wood or a sack of meal, it was true, but the pastor's family was one of the poorest in the community.

He saw Christine cast a wistful glance at the loom in the corner of the room. Samuel gave her free use of his deceased wife's loom and spinning wheel. Christine had shown a talent for weaving soon after her arrival two years earlier. She had learned the craft from the nuns at the convent in Canada where she'd lived for four years. Of course, they both knew she wouldn't be weaving on Sunday.

Samuel turned his attention to the meal—a simple stew, corn bread baked yesterday, and the promise of gingerbread after. The spicy smell of ginger tantalized them all from beneath one of Goody Deane's threadbare linen towels.

He didn't like to recall Christine's background or the events that had brought her into contact with his family. A number of the village's residents had been captured by Indians, either at the massacre of 1689 or in other raids. Several members of the Otis and Dudley families, as well as Charles and Jane Gardner, were survivors of captivity. Busybodies set rumors flying about the conditions under which the captives had lived and the state of their souls as a result. But none of the others had lived in a nunnery for years, as Christine had. The people of Cochecho had accepted most of the redeemed captives back into their ranks, but he knew a few still looked on Christine with suspicion because of her years at the convent.

He saw growing acceptance as Christine attended church faithfully and performed good deeds with a self-effacing humility. Most of the prominent women of the community now treated her well. Samuel's close contact with her had taught him that her faith was firm, and her love and tender care for his children was exceeded only by that which their own mother had bestowed. Christine was indeed a blessing to their family.

"Will you have some greens?" Goody Deane stood at Christine's elbow with a wooden bowl of boiled greens the girls had gathered at the edge of the woods on Saturday.

"Aye, thank you." Christine held her plate up.

"We'll be eating corn from the garden soon." Pastor Jewett set the kettle of steaming water for the dishes aside and raked the coals into a heap on the stone hearth. He covered them with ashes, banking them. They didn't want to keep burning wood all afternoon since it was now very warm in the house, but they would want the live coals later, when it was time to cook supper.

"Yes, and cucumbers, too." Goody Deane put a small portion of greens on each of the girls' plates.

"I can't wait for fresh corn." Constance rubbed her tummy. They all laughed.

"Me, either," Christine said. All that was left of last year's crop was dry ground corn and a barrel of parched corn kernels, and those supplies were dwindling. "It will be a little while longer before we get corn, though." The summer garden supplied them with plenty of green beans, leaf lettuce, and tender carrots and beets. This time of year, the Jewetts ate as well as most other families in Cochecho.

Samuel sat down and opened his Bible on his knees. He wanted to refresh his mind for the afternoon sermon.

When Christine and the girls had eaten and washed and put away their dishes, Goody Deane threw out the dishwater, and Christine put Ruth on her pallet for a nap.

"There, now," Christine said to Abby and Constance, "Goody Deane and I shall see you at worship. We'll go home now for a short rest. Be good girls, won't you?"

"I be going to call on Richard Otis after the service this

afternoon, to see how he is recovering from his wounds," Samuel said.

Christine straightened and looked at him. "Do you wish me to stay with the children then?"

He hesitated. Richard Otis, the blacksmith whose father had been killed in the massacre six years earlier, was one who had suffered grievous wounds in the attack two weeks ago. Since that fray, the elders had posted a lookout on the meeting-house steps during each service. But the parsonage lay in the middle of the village, and he would not be gone long this evening. If the service did not run overly long, he could be home before dark. "Nay. You've done so much. There's no fire hazard, and Ben is a responsible enough lad to watch his sisters for a couple of hours. Eh, son?"

Ben grimaced. "Yes, Father."

Samuel stood and ruffled the boy's hair. "Good lad."

Christine hung up her apron and glanced once more toward the loom. She couldn't work at her weaving today. In fact, scripture bade them do no more work than they found absolutely necessary on Sunday. Samuel strictly enforced the Sabbath rest in his household. He knew Christine understood this, but still, her plain features took on a wistfulness when she regarded the loom.

"Let me walk you ladies home," he said. "I'd like a word with you, Miss Hardin." He was not usually so formal with her except in public, but the matter he needed to discuss was a serious one.

Christine raised her eyebrows but said nothing.

After the three had crossed the road together, he paused on Goody Deane's path.

Christine halted as well and waited for him to speak.

"Constance tells me Goody Ackley asked you to work for her," he said.

Christine looked down at the ground. "Aye. But I declined her offer."

Goody Deane swung around near the doorstone. "I'll be stretching out yonder if you need me, Christine. Thank you kindly for the vittles, Parson."

"And thank you for bringing the gingerbread, ma'am. It added a festive note to our Sabbath-day dinner."

"Ah, well, a bit of gingerbread never went down wrong, I say." Goody Deane nodded and went into the cottage.

Samuel cleared his throat and met Christine's gaze. "If I could pay you in coin, I would. You know that. Your labor in my house has been worth much more than I've been able to give you. But I expect the Ackleys would give you a fair wage, and if you—"

Christine's hazel eyes grew large as he spoke, and her brow puckered. "Please, Pastor, do not speak of it. I do not wish to go to the Ackleys', and I'm happy with our arrangement."

He exhaled and smiled. "Bless you. But the Ackleys would give you room in their loft, I'm sure. The last hired girl had a place there."

"I enjoy living with Goody Deane, and I think I do not boast to say she likes having me."

"Oh, to be sure," he said quickly. "I've thought it good for her since the beginning. I'm certain you are a great help to her, and she seems in much better spirits since you've boarded with her."

Christine nodded. "A pleasant situation and a congenial employer go further than a generous wage, sir. And I'm not sure how generous the goodwife we speak of would be."

Samuel couldn't refute that. He'd heard Goody Ackley wrangled over the last ha'penny with the trader, and her husband, Roger Ackley, was well known to be a skinflint. But even the stingiest couple in Cochecho would probably pay Christine more than he could. He rarely gave her a coin. He did allow her to sell cloth that she wove on his loom and keep the profit, but most of the textiles she produced seemed to find themselves clothing his own children.

"When it comes down to it, I don't give you much for your labor."

"Ah, well"—she looked down once more, and her cheeks flushed—"you give me all I need, sir. My food and any other necessities. And you've allowed me to be a part of your family, which is a great boon."

They stood in silence for a moment. Samuel tried to imagine the family now without Christine. A brief image of domestic chaos and wailing children flickered across his mind. "You truly do not wish to go to the Ackleys' farm, then?"

"I do not." She looked up and gazed at him earnestly, her plain features less serene than usual. "If you are happy, I should like to continue things as they are."

"We agree then. I shall see you in half an hour, at meeting."

Samuel tipped his hat and turned toward the street.

two

A week later, Christine spent a good part of Monday morning working in Goody Deane's garden. The pastor had suggested in the spring that they plant enough vegetables at the parsonage for Christine and Goody Deane as well as the Jewett family, and Tabitha Deane's small plot was now given over to herbs. Christine had invited the three little girls to help her weed the small garden and pick mint, yarrow, and basil leaves for drying. Ruth and Constance took to the work eagerly.

"Why don't you sit in the shade now with your dollies?" Christine asked when they had picked all the herbs she wanted for the present. "I shall finish placing stones along the path here. You girls may play for a while, and then I shall fix us a cup of mint tea."

The two girls retrieved their rag dolls from the back stoop. Christine had fashioned Ruth's doll from scraps, modeling it from the design of the ones Elizabeth Jewett had stitched for her two older daughters. Now Ruth's doll, Lucy, was never far from her. She had cried the first time her father told her that Lucy could not go to church with her, but Abby had calmed her and whispered to her that their dolls would go to "doll meeting" while the real people were away. Ever since, Ruth had happily dressed Lucy in her best gown and shawl on Sunday mornings and left her sitting on Mother's chair beside Abby's and Constance's dolls when they left for the meetinghouse. Stories about "doll meeting" were now favorite bedtime tales.

After a quarter hour's hard work on the stone walkway, Christine looked up to see Goody Deane and Abby Jewett returning from their excursion to the trading post. While Christine disliked going out among people, Goody Deane enjoyed socializing. When her joints didn't ache too badly, she would happily undertake errands while Christine dealt with cleaning. Christine had permitted Abby to accompany her on her excursion that morning.

"Miss Christine," Abby cried when she spotted her in the garden. She ran up the path, clutching the handle of the small basket Goody Deane had entrusted to her. "We got the black buttons you asked for and a bottle of ink for Father!"

"Lovely." Christine straightened and pressed her hands to the small of her back. Being tall had its disadvantages. "You two are just in time to join us for a cup of tea."

The widow had by this time reached them. "Bless you. I can use it." She pulled a snowy handkerchief from the sleeve of her brown linsey gown and wiped her brow. "I shall remember this heat next winter when I'm shivering. Remind me if I complain about the cold."

Christine laughed and gathered her tools. "Come, Ruthie. Constance, time for tea."

They all went inside, and Christine stirred the embers in the fireplace while Goody Deane hung up her bonnet.

"There, now," Christine said. "I'll fix the tea, and you can get a loaf of that new bread, Abby. We'll all have a slice."

The girl headed for the worktable near the window where two loaves of crusty brown bread awaited her. The widow had risen early, set her bread, and had it baked and cooling before she ever left for the trading post.

"Goody Deane?" Abby's voice rose in uncertainty.

"What is it, child? I shall fetch the knife, is that it?"

"Nay." Abby turned and looked at Christine and the widow.

"Were there not three loaves when we left this morn?"

Christine and Tabitha Deane stepped toward the table.

"To be sure," said Goody Deane. "Miss Christine must have put one away."

Christine shook her head. "Not I."

"Well. Isn't that strange? I'm sure we had three. But sometimes I get addled."

"Nay, you remember correctly." Christine looked on the floor and at the shelves on the nearby wall. "Where do you suppose it got to?"

Constance and Ruth came over to stare at the two remaining loaves.

"Perhaps it's with Mr. Heard's shirt," Abby offered.

"How is that?" Christine glanced at her keenly.

Goody Deane waved a hand through the air. "Ah, she heard it told at the trader's how Mrs. Heard missed her husband's second-best shirt off the clothesline last washday." The widow drew in a quick breath. "Perhaps there's some sense in that, though, Abby. After all, when Mrs. Heard told it, Goody Ackley chimed in with a tale of a missing roast of lamb."

Abby nodded solemnly, her wide brown eyes still on the loaves.

"Well, come on," Christine said briskly. "Let's have a slice of this good bread before it walks off on us."

She poured hot water over the crushed mint leaves, and Goody Deane set about cutting the bread. Christine took down the only two cups in the house, a chipped saucer, a small pannikin, and a custard dish. The girls wouldn't mind drinking out of the odd assortment of dishes. At last each was settled about the table with a thick slice of the good rye bread before her, slathered in butter that Sarah Dudley had brought them on Sunday.

"I believe young Mrs. Dudley makes the best butter I've ever tasted." Goody Deane smacked her lips.

"Aye, Sarah has a fair hand with it. She says it's because of all the clover in the field where their cow grazes." Christine reached over to tuck a linen towel securely in the neckband of Ruth's dress.

"Goody Ackley was rude today." Abby licked a smear of butter off her fingers.

"Really, Abby. Let us be kind," Christine said gently.

"She be honest," Goody Deane said. "That woman was rude, indeed, but it were nothing new."

Christine inhaled slowly, wondering how she could teach the girls not to gossip if their hostess encouraged it.

"Who did she rude to?" Ruth asked.

"To whom was she rude," Christine murmured.

"Aye." Ruth nodded vigorously, and Christine had to smile.

"Goodman Ackley." Abby took a big bite of her bread and butter.

"Her husband?" Christine eyed Abby then shot a glance at Goody Deane.

"As I said, nothing new in these parts." The widow sipped her tea. "Roger Ackley was with her, and she kept needling him about this and that, things she needed that he seemed reluctant to buy. I heard him say once that something could wait until after harvest, but the wife went on about how she always has to wait, wait, wait. So he put it on credit." Goody Deane shook her head. "And she treats the trader's clerk shamefully. She as much as accused him of cheating her this morning, but when the coins were laid out and counted, the clerk was in the right."

"Well." Christine didn't know what else to say.

"Aye. But did she apologize?" the widow asked.

"She did not," Abby cried, her eyes glittering. "She scooped up the pennies and said, 'Hmpf.'"

Christine held back a giggle. She reached for her cup to give herself a chance to recover her decorum. After a sip, she said, "Well, perhaps we should introduce a new topic."

"Do you be going over to the parsonage today?" Tabitha asked.

"Aye." Christine glanced at the window and noted how the sunlight shone through from nearly overhead. "It's getting on for noon. I must go over and get dinner on."

"Father will be home from church soon." Abby jumped down off her bench and ran to fetch her doll.

"He could do his studying at home, now that they have the two new rooms," Christine said.

"But people would talk if you spent the day there while he was home," the widow reminded her.

It was true. She couldn't stay at the parsonage all the time, especially when the master of the house was in it. Though she had lived there while Elizabeth was alive, that was no longer acceptable. When the pastor's wife died, Goody Deane had offered her a bed in her cottage across the way, and she often accompanied Christine to lend an added air of propriety.

"I can go with you," Goody Deane said.

"You are far too kind. Don't you have things you wish to do here?"

"Nay. You keep this little place so tidy, I've naught to put my hands to. But the children always have washing and mending to be done at the parsonage, and one can never bake enough corn pone to keep those boys sated."

Christine patted her hand. "Thank you. If you wish to come over later and do some mending and perhaps stir up some biscuits, I might put an hour in at the loom. I'm nearly done with that length of linen, and I'd like to warp some black woolen soon."

"The boys be outgrowing their togs?"

"I'd like to weave enough for new trousers for both John and Ben, and their father's winter coat is disgracefully shabby. I hope he'll have a new coat before snow falls again in New Hampshire."

Goody Deane brushed the crumbs off the table into her apron. "Be Sarah Dudley giving you the wool?"

"Aye, she traded me a great quantity for Ben's work at planting time. Well, she traded with the pastor and Ben, that is."

"She's a good soul." Tabitha frowned as she covered the remaining bread in a towel. "I do wonder where that loaf of bread got to. We might have to bake again before the week is out."

&

"Move along, John. We haven't all day." Samuel hastened to fill the woodbox, while the boys carried water and fed the few chickens that scratched the backyard bare.

When he returned to the house with his last load of firewood, Christine was tying Ruth's skirt on over her diminutive cotton shift. Constance sat on the bench by the table. Abby knelt before her, wielding the buttonhook.

"Almost ready, Father," Abby called as he dropped his wood into the woodbox.

"Good girl."

Christine caught his eye, and he smiled at her over Ruth's head. They *were* good children. Well behaved and diligent. Since their mother's passing, Christine had proved trustworthy to continue their training. She even did a bit of spelling and ciphering with Abby and Constance on mornings when John and Ben joined him at the church for their lessons. He would have to talk to her before harvest to see what she thought about the dame school Mrs. Otis planned to start. It would ease Christine's burdens a mite to have the two girls out from underfoot a few hours each day. Still, she didn't seem to mind having them about.

"We're ready," Constance cried, jumping off the bench. She stumbled forward, toward the hearth, and Samuel reached out just in time to catch her.

"Careful, now. Even though the fire's banked, you could get hurt badly if you fly into the hearth."

"Yes, Father."

He locked eyes with her and nodded sternly before releasing her. Cooking and scalding accidents accounted for many deaths among the women and children of the colony, and he demanded caution in the kitchen. In his capacity as makeshift healer, he'd seen too many charred bodies. If he could help it, his children would never be among them.

"Will we get to see Catherine?" Abby asked as they left the parsonage.

"Perchance," Samuel said. His girls had a fondness for Catherine Dudley, Sarah's young sister-in-law, who often told them stories and brought them treats. "My purpose is to visit her parents today and see what their needs be and to make arrangement with Goodman Dudley about the work he needs from Ben."

"And we ladies shall call on Sarah Dudley and Jane Gardner as well," Christine said.

The searing August sun already baked through Samuel's clothing. He rarely went about without his coat, but the weather had given him pause. Would he rather be thought a proper parson and risk taking ill from the heat, or seem informal to his parishioners and live to tell about it? He had compromised on a waistcoat over his best linen shirt. He hung his powder horn and bullet pouch over his shoulder, hoisted his musket, and swung Ruth up with his other arm. "Come, littlest. We shall make better progress if I carry you."

As they traversed the path between the village and James Dudley's palisaded compound, he considered the progress his family had made since Elizabeth's death and that of their infant son at the end of March the year before. The rift was still fresh in his heart, but they had fallen into new routines and habits, made easier by Christine's ministrations.

She was a capable housekeeper and a gentle caregiver for the children, though she exacted obedience from them. *Too bad she doesn't wish to marry,* he mused. Christine might make a natural mother. But she had voiced her disinclination to marry and bear children several times to his wife, back when she lived at the parsonage. He was sure her captivity and her years in the nunnery had strengthened those feelings. She seemed content to work for a family not her own, to the point of exhausting herself. He recalled how ill she had been after she and Jane cared for his family during the smallpox epidemic.

Although most grateful for her selflessness, he desired to make things easier for her. He supposed the best thing he could actually do to lighten Christine's burdens would be to remarry. Then she could go and work for someone else for real wages. Or, if she preferred to stay on, she could at least share the labor with the mistress of the house.

The thought made his head swim. Some men remarried quickly after being widowed, with Mordecai Wales a case in point. But the idea of taking another woman as his wife repelled Samuel. Elizabeth had been his joy, and she was gone little more than a year.

I'm nowhere near ready for that.

No, it was not to be considered. He squared his shoulders, relieved to have faced the thought.

All in Your time, heavenly Father.

As they passed Roger Ackley's farm, he heard the good-wife's shrill voice through the open window of the house.

"Mr. Ackley! Mi–i–i–ister Ackley! Where be that tub of water you promised to fetch me for washing?"

Christine looked askance at him, and Samuel shrugged.

"I hear Alice Stevens is going to start working for the Ackleys soon." Privately, he questioned how long that would last. If Mahalia Ackley treated her maids the same way she treated her husband, it was no wonder she couldn't keep domestic help.

They trudged on, and when they were past the house, he could see Goodman Ackley toiling toward the side door, pushing a wheelbarrow that held a squatty barrel Samuel assumed was full of wash water.

If the children had not been along, he would have stopped to have a word with the couple, but he had no desire to expose his family to the farm wife's critical eye. He had heard the damage her tongue could do all too often. He wouldn't want her telling others, for instance, that Abby's skirt was scandalously short. Why hadn't he noticed before how tall she was getting? Perhaps Christine could make over one of Elizabeth's old skirts for his eldest daughter.

James Dudley and his sons were in the hayfield when the Jewetts and Christine approached. James and Richard sliced the tall grass with sweeping cuts, while Stephen stood guard with a musket.

Samuel had no doubt the other two had guns lying close at hand as they worked. He lowered Ruth to the ground and let her walk with Christine and the older girls toward the gate in the fence surrounding the garrison house. He walked into the field with John and Ben. The smell of the newly cut hay hung in the hot air. "A fine crop you'll have," he called to James as he neared his host.

"Aye, thank ye. That we shall, if the rain holds off."

"The Lord willing, it shall come when needed," Samuel

said with a smile. "We're later than I'd planned. Forgive me. But Ben brought our scythe along."

James shrugged. "It takes a big family time to pack and remove. I should be shocked if you arrived at dawn with all the young'uns in tow." He leaned for a moment on his scythe handle and wiped his brow with a kerchief. "I allow Catherine and my wife will be glad to see all your womenfolk."

Samuel waved to Stephen, who waved back and returned to scanning the edges of the field. "Any sign of Indians?"

"Not since that fracas after meeting a fortnight past," James Dudley replied.

Samuel nodded. "They usually come at night or early morn. You're probably safe."

"But you never know." Dudley lifted his scythe and swung viciously at the tall grass.

❧

By the time they left for their walk back to the parsonage in midafternoon, Christine's fatigue oppressed her. She had spent much of the day on her feet, spinning wool for Jane and helping her churn butter. Catherine and Sarah had joined them, and all had shared in the cleaning and baking. At the end of their visit, Jane had two pounds of fresh butter—she sent one back with the Jewetts—two skeins of fine gray woolen yarn, two berry pies, and enough newly baked bread to last her and Charles a week.

The smell of the baking loaves had prompted Abby to tell the ladies about the disappearing bread at Goody Deane's house. Christine had confirmed her story.

"Likely Goody Deane was confused," Sarah said. "She is getting on in years."

"Nay, she baked three loaves, of that I'm certain." Christine shook her head. "I hate to think someone stole one."

"It wouldn't surprise me," Catherine said. "I had a row of

beans almost ready to pick last week, in the bed just outside the palisade. I went out one morning to pick them for dinner, and what think ye? Someone had stripped the vines before I came. Fair tasting them, I was."

"You didn't tell me," Sarah said, her blue eyes narrowed.

"Someone picked them off before you?" Jane asked.

"Aye. I asked Father and Mother and Stephen, but none of them had done it."

"Perhaps a deer got them," Christine suggested.

"Nay, they would have eaten the plants right off. These were very neatly picked. Father said to be watchful for savages, but we never saw any."

Christine kept a sharp eye during their walk home, but no mishaps befell them.

"You needn't tend our supper tonight," the pastor said as they approached the village. You're fatigued. Go home and enjoy the rest of the day with Goody Deane."

"Who will feed us?" Constance asked, staring up at her father.

"I shall do it. Even a man as clumsy as myself can build up the fire under the stewpot and set out the biscuits Miss Christine put by last night. And you and Abby shall help me."

"And there be mince pie left," said John, licking his chapped lips.

"We can fend for ourselves," Samuel said with a smile.

Christine returned his smile. "I'm sure you can, but I'd like to come and weave for a while, if you don't mind, before the light is gone."

She did just that, managing to finish the linen that she and the pastor had agreed she could sell.

"That's nice work, Christine," he said as she carefully folded the material. "You have a buyer already, I believe?"

"Mrs. Heard told me last spring she would take any linen

I could give her, after she saw the sheeting I wove for Mrs. Otis."

The pastor nodded. "Aye. And you shall keep the price."

"Nay, sir. You supplied the flax and the loom."

"We have had this conversation before. Without your labor, there would be no linen."

She inhaled deeply. "Then, sir, if you insist, we shall split the profit." She glanced at the children and lowered her voice. "I don't like to say it, sir, but Ben at least will need new boots in the fall. All of the children are growing quickly, and—"

"I fear you are right. I noticed today how tall Abby is getting. Think you that one of my wife's skirts could be cut down for her?"

It was the practical thing to do, of course. "Certainly. I'll see to it tomorrow."

He nodded. "Very well, then, we shall go halves. My portion of the linen money shall go to the cobbler and to the trader for whatever foodstuffs you think we need. But your part is yours to keep and do with as you wish."

She could see that he would brook no further argument, so she lowered her chin. All too stubborn that chin had become lately, she supposed. Sometimes it felt as if these were her own children she championed. "We agree, sir."

"Good. Now, you must be on your way. I insist that we shall make our own supper tonight."

She opened her mouth to protest, but Ben chimed in with, "I'll make up the fire, Father, and John will help Abby set the table."

John threw a dark look at his brother, but the pastor's features relaxed.

Christine decided it might be well for him to have a calm evening alone with his children. She had left the stew ready to heat in the iron kettle, and there really wasn't much to do.

"Thank you," she said. "I expect Goody Deane and I shall retire early." She gathered her things and crossed the dusty street to the widow's cottage.

As she opened the door, Goody Deane startled in her chair, and Christine greeted her softly. "Good evening. The pastor says he and the children can take care of themselves tonight."

"I been looking for ye to come back," the old woman said. "If I'd known ye weren't eating at the parson's, I'd have put supper on."

"Don't stir yourself," Christine told her. "It looks as though you've made a lot of progress on your knitting today. I'll build the fire up and fix us a bite."

"Oh, do we need to heat the house up? It's just now getting bearable. I have hopes of a restful sleep tonight, but not if we get the fire up and heat the house to a simmer."

"Very well." Christine opened the tin box where they kept bread and remnants of food. "I think there's enough lamb here to eke out a meal with bread and butter, and I spy a morsel of seed cake. I'll fetch a bucket of cool water, and we'll sit down."

She took up the nearly empty water pail and dumped the little that was in it into a pitcher. The cottage had no well, but the walk to the river was a short one. It took her only a few minutes to reach the bank and fill her bucket.

The trader's daughter had also come to fetch water, and they greeted each other cheerfully.

Christine trudged alone back to the little house, thinking about her place in the community. When she first returned from her captivity in Canada, she had felt like an outsider and was shunned by many of the villagers. But time and contact had softened their attitudes, and she now felt a part of Cochecho. Her pleasant days divided between Goody Deane's cottage and the parsonage filled her with contentment.

She was nearly to the cottage door when she saw a dark figure flit across the garden in the twilight, toward the back of the house. Christine halted so quickly that water sloshed over the rim of the bucket, soaking the bottom of her skirt. She set the pail down quietly in the path and tiptoed to the corner of the house.

A man in ragged clothes was peering in Goody Deane's kitchen window. He turned toward her, his eyes wide.

Before she could speak, he gestured threateningly. "Quiet, miss. If ye give alarm, I'll kill ye."

three

Samuel served his children supper and was about to sit down to his own plate of food, when a peremptory knocking sounded on the door.

Edward Chapman, one of the fishermen who lived along the riverbank, stood outside, panting as though he had run all the way from his house. His rapid breathing and unsteady gaze told Samuel immediately that something untoward had happened.

"Edward! What's the trouble?"

"Parson, can you come? The cow kicked my boy, Philip, and I think his knee is broken."

"The poor lad. I'll come take a look." Samuel looked around, swiftly taking a mental count of the children. "Ben, I shall be gone for an hour or two. Read a chapter with the children and send the girls to bed. Abby, you will have to help Ruth undress."

"Might I stay up with Ben, Father?" John asked.

"Aye. And if you need any help, run over the way for Miss Christine."

Ben picked up Ruth and her doll from the rag rug. "We'll be fine."

"Here, Father. Take this with you." Abby ran to the table and plucked a biscuit from his untouched plate.

Samuel smiled and accepted it from her. "Thank you, Abby, dear. Be good and help put the dishes to rights, won't you? But let Ben pour the hot water."

He went out into the dusk with Chapman, shoving the

biscuit into his pocket. As they walked, he sought to calm the worried father. "Be Philip in sore distress?"

"Aye, sir. He bellowed like a cow moose. Awful pain."

Samuel shook his head. "I'm sorry, Edward. I hope one day a physician will feel called to settle here among us. My ministrations are far from expert."

"You've a better touch than anyone else in the village, and twice the heart."

Samuel bowed his head and sent up a prayer for wisdom beyond his skill. Lately it seemed his theological studies were interrupted more and more often. Of course, summer brought more accidents with all of the farming activity.

Word had gotten about the first year he and Elizabeth moved to Cochecho, after he stitched up a man's gashed scalp. The new preacher was as good as a doctor, some insisted. Samuel knew better. He acted because someone had to, and so they believed he had a special aptitude for it. As the village grew, so did the calls for his medical assistance. When he could, he steered people to Captain Baldwin's wife, who acted as midwife and herb woman. But serious injuries were beyond her, she'd told him early, though she often helped nurse Samuel's patients after he had done what he could.

Chapman seemed calmer by the time they came in sight of his cottage near the river. "I expect the boy will be fine once you set his leg," he said.

Samuel nodded. "Let us pray so. If it needs setting, I'll have you fetch me the splints."

"I can do that."

"Good. How has your catch been this summer?"

"The Lord has been quite generous," Chapman said. "I've been out on the boat much of the time. By chance I was home tonight when the boy went to milk the cow."

"God knew you would be needed," Samuel said.

They reached the path to the house. "Well, he's quit scream-ing," Edward noted. "I made sure I was home ere nightfall. The wife says there's been pilfering in the neighborhood. Like as not, some Indians are skulking about, she says."

"I've heard as much from some others," Samuel admitted. "I have no explanation. . .but I've heard of no raids or attacks since the one at the church. Just small things gone missing. Food, mostly."

As Chapman opened the door, he heard weeping, and the fisherman's wife cried, "Bless you, Parson! Our boy is in bad straits. I told him you would come and make it better."

Samuel winced, wishing he had a stock of medicines and a physician's manual. But God had called him to be a minister, not a doctor. He closed the door firmly and smiled at Mrs. Chapman. "I will do my best, ma'am. Have you any comfrey or boneset?"

❧

"What do you want?" Christine's voice croaked. Her heart drummed as though it would leap out of her chest.

The man stood in shadows, with his bearded face muffled in darkness. The pale skin below his eyes stood out, and as he shifted, she caught a metallic glint in his right hand.

"Don't you yell."

"I won't." Christine bit her bottom lip to still its trembling.

He raised the knife just a bit, making sure she saw it. "If you squawk, you've had it, that's all."

She nodded.

"Good, then. Bring me something to eat."

"We. . .don't have much."

"Oh, I know. I've seen you go back and forth to the house over yonder. But you keep food here, too. Here, where there's no kids snooping around. That's why I came here and not there. I thought I had a better chance to get somewhat to eat without anyone seeing me."

Christine shivered, though the evening breeze was warm. "Did you steal our loaf of bread yesterday?"

He smiled, and she could see his white teeth grinning ghoulishly in the fading light. "Aye, and good bread it were. I know you ladies can cook, that I do. I says to myself, 'This 'ere loaf will last a long time.' But it was so tasty, and I was like to starve. I ate it all yesterday, that I did."

"I can't steal from Goody Deane. She's a poor woman and she doesn't have much."

"She's got more than me." His lips drew back in a snarl, and he moved the knife. "Bring me some vittles, woman. You hear?"

Christine gulped for air. Would she ever be able to draw a full breath again? Her lungs felt as though a giant squeezed them. "I'll try."

"See that you do. And don't you tell the old crone." He laid a hand on her arm, heavy and warm through her sleeve.

Christine yanked away, and he chuckled.

"Think about it, now. If you tell that old woman—or anyone else—I'll see that you regret it."

"I'm not afraid of you." She threw back her shoulders, hoping he hadn't caught the tremor in her voice.

"Oh, you're not? Well then, I'll have to see that you are. You need to respect me because I will act if you don't do as I say."

"What will you do?" She meant it to come out strong and sneering, but her dread was all too apparent in the low, shaky words.

He smiled again and held the knife up, trying the edge of its four-inch blade with his thumb. "Those pretty little girls what live yonder. . ." He jerked his head toward the Reverend Jewett's home. "I'll make one of them not so pretty. Y'hear?"

She jumped at his growl and stepped back. "Y–yes. I'll bring you something."

"That's a good lass. Bring me some of that cake I smelt cooking earlier."

"I don't know about any cake. I've been gone all day."

"Oh, I know, I know. But there was cake, and she won't have eaten it all."

A shiver snaked down Christine's spine. How close had he ventured to where Goody Deane worked? Just beneath the window? And for how many days had he spied on them? She had no doubt that he would make good his threats if she did not do as he asked.

"Where shall I bring it?"

"Christine?" The widow's quavering voice floated through the window and across the sultry air. "Is that you, Christine Hardin?"

"Answer," the man hissed.

"I'm coming."

"When she's abed, you come," he said. "Take it out back, near the necessary. I'll be waiting." He faded into the twilight.

Christine hurried to where she had left the bucket of water. She hefted it and bunched up a handful of her skirt, lifting the hem a couple of inches. She hobbled into the house as quickly as she could without spilling more water.

Goody Deane stood just inside the door, holding the poker in her hand.

"What kept you, child? I thought I heard a man's voice."

"Oh, a man did greet me in passing." Christine turned away from her and hid her face while she poured water into the teakettle. She drew the muslin curtains, wondering if the stranger was watching and listening. She wished she dared put up the shutters, but Goody Deane would complain about the heat.

"What man?"

Christine froze for an instant. She couldn't lie. But what

could she say? She made her hands resume their labor. "Oh, it was. . .just a man passing by."

"Did he want to call?"

"Oh, no, no, nothing like that." How awful if Goody Deane had the mistaken impression that Christine had a suitor and tried to hide it from her. "Trust me, dear lady, I shall tell you if we have gentleman callers."

Goody Deane smiled. "You never know. Now, what will it be? I baked a little honey cake today."

"Lovely. But we must have some cheese first and a slice of bread." Even as she spoke, she wondered if she could save the small portion of lamb for the stranger.

She sat down at the table a moment later with Tabitha Deane and managed to choke down her supper.

If only she could tell someone. But whom? The Reverend Jewett seemed most logical. His children were the ones threatened by this criminal. Did she dare? If she told anyone, the outlaw would retaliate. She mulled over his words, his tone, his manner, and decided she indeed believed he would carry out his threats.

When at last the widow was abed and snoring gently, Christine tiptoed to the tin box and removed the small amount of meat left there and two generous slices of bread. They had no fresh vegetables in the house, but she had no doubt the man was helping himself to those from her neighbors' gardens as quickly as they ripened.

She lit a candle in a pierced tin lantern and carefully opened the door. She ought to have put some grease on those hinges.

Outside on the flat stone before the door, she waited half a minute, listening. She almost wished Tabitha would start up and call to her again, but all was silent within. The cricket choir chirped, and the warm breeze rustled the leaves of the maple trees.

She set out slowly along the path through the herb garden, around the side of the house. Each step seemed more difficult. Madness, meeting a violent man alone in the night.

Lord, give me safe passage there and back!

The little building stood just within the tree line, a discreet distance from the cottage, but too far for Christine's liking. If she screamed for help, would her voice penetrate the widow's slumber?

She stopped, eyeing the tiny shed. The door was off the latch. He wouldn't be inside, would he?

"So, ye came."

She jumped and whirled to face a black shape emerging from the trees.

"Y—yes. I said I would."

He gave a snort of a laugh. "So ye did. Ye can be sure I was watching to see if you went out again tonight. If you'd gone anywhere but here, I'd have known."

She shivered, wanting nothing more than to get away from him. "Here." She held out the tin plate with the food on it. "It's all I could get. It's not much, and the widow might question me about it even so."

He took the plate and shoved a piece of the meat into his mouth. "You've saved a man's life, miss." She could barely make out the words, garbled as they were with his chewing.

"I doubt that," she said. "You'd have found sustenance somewhere. I only made it easier for you and less likely you'd be caught."

"That's right. This ain't stealin', now, is it? You gave me these vittles."

She didn't deign to reply.

"I'm not so bad. Truly, I'm not. I'm innocent, you know?"

"Of what?" She wished she hadn't responded, but he'd piqued her curiosity.

"They run me out of Haverhill, they did. Said I done something terrible, but I was innocent. I went to trial, and they couldn't prove anything on me, but they still made me leave. The magistrate banished me from the township. I went to Portsmouth, but they heard about me from folks in Haverhill, and they said the same. 'Go peaceful, or we'll lock you up for vagrancy.' But I'm innocent of the charges, I tell you."

She wanted to ask what the charges were but decided she might be better off not knowing. She turned away.

"Wait!" he called, his mouth full again.

She paused and turned back unwillingly.

"You'll need the plate."

"Leave it on the step. I'll get it in the morning."

"Oh, I can do better than that. The old woman might go out early and step on it there. Nay, I'll set it up on the window ledge, behind those pretty white curtains. When you get up, you can reach out and get it ever so easy. And bring me a blanket. Sure, it's warm tonight, but it might turn cool tomorrow."

She eyed his dark silhouette for a moment. He picked up a slice of bread and folded it, sticking half of it in his mouth. She left him, walking quickly down the path without looking back.

four

In the morning Christine found the plate, as promised, on the window ledge. She took it in, washed it, and used it in setting the breakfast table before Goody Deane was finished dressing. The old woman's gnarled hands made it difficult for her to button and tie her clothing, but she didn't want to give up trying. Usually she managed, albeit slowly.

"I believe I'll go over to the Jewetts' with you today," the widow said.

"You'll be welcome. I plan to do a wash and begin weaving that wool. If there's anything ready in the garden, you and the children can pick it."

"Aye, and pluck a few weeds." Tabitha eyed her hands. "As long as God allows, I'll keep on being useful."

Christine was thankful that Tabitha had decided to go. Otherwise, she probably would have fretted all day, wondering if the stranger hung about and Tabitha were in danger. Of course, with the cottage empty, he might go in and help himself to whatever he could find. She refused to dwell on the unwelcome thought.

By the time the two women arrived at the parsonage, Pastor Jewett had already left with John to take Christine's linen to the Heard garrison and visit his patients at the Chapman and Otis houses. Christine set to work with a sense of relief. His absence settled the nagging question of whether or not to tell him about her encounter with the outlaw.

"You should have fetched me last night," she said, when Ben told her about Chapman's call for his father the evening

39

before. "I could have come back."

"Nay, we were fine. Except Connie cried because there was no more mince pie."

"What? I thought half a pie was left."

"So we thought, but when John went to get it down, there was only one small piece left." Ben shrugged. "Of course, we had to leave it for Father."

"Of course." Christine walked to the pie safe on the shelf and opened it. The tin box was now empty.

"Father said when he came home that mayhap you—" Ben stopped and looked away.

"What?"

He winced. "He said mayhap you took it home for you and Goody Deane."

"I did no such thing."

"We had a cake of our own yesterday, and no mince pies," the widow chimed in, glaring at Ben.

"I didn't really think it." Ben kicked at a piece of bark on the hearth. "Do you want the fire built up?"

"I think we'd better," Christine said.

Goody Deane nodded, her eyes snapping. "Aye, it sounds as though we'd best make some mincemeat pies for this rabble."

"Oh, you don't need to—"

"Hush, Ben," Christine said with a smile. "She's only teasing you. Fetch some good, dry wood and get a new crock of mincemeat from the root cellar."

"There be only one left."

"Ah, well, soon we'll have apples to make more, won't we?"

"Not for a good month," Goody Deane said.

"I know where there be blackberries," Abby piped up from the corner where she sat with her sampler. "May we go and pick some, Miss Christine?"

The thought of the outlaw crossed her mind. "Oh, I think not."

"They're only out behind the church," Ben said. "I'll take the girls, if you like."

She turned that over in her mind. They would be easily visible from the common, and easily heard if Ben called for help. Still, she had no doubt the thief had been inside the parsonage while the family was at the Dudleys' the previous day. "Very well, but leave Ruth here with me. "Ben, you must watch the girls, and beware of strangers, won't you?"

He cocked his head to one side in a gesture that imitated his father exactly. "Aye."

She helped them get ready, wondering if she were making a costly mistake. She tied Constance's bonnet strings firmly and put a small pail in her hands.

"You will be careful of them, Ben?"

"You can be sure of it, Miss Christine."

She leaned toward him and whispered, "All this pilfering, you know. There may be someone lurking about."

His eyes widened. "You mean—the pie?"

"Well, we don't know, do we?"

He nodded gravely and hustled the two girls out the door.

While they were gone, Christine went through the parsonage larder. She thought there were fewer raisins than there had been, but John was known to sneak a handful now and then. The height of the beechnuts in their jar seemed lower, but she couldn't be sure. She simply couldn't tell if the outlaw had stolen more than two or three pieces of pie, but she had no doubt in her mind that he had rifled the Jewetts' stores while they were gone. He had certainly had more to eat than that loaf of Goody Deane's bread on Monday.

She looked about the main room. He knew the arrangement of the house now and where the children slept. It made her skin crawl. "I shouldn't have let them go."

"What?" Tabitha Deane asked.

"The children. I should have made them wait until their father returned."

"It's only behind the meetinghouse."

"I know."

"Go with them, then. They'll pick their berries quicker and be home in half an hour. I'll watch Ruth and start preparing the crust."

Christine untied her apron and hung it up. "You think I'm silly, don't you?" She grabbed an iron kettle with a bail handle.

"Nay. You speak as a mother would."

She dashed out the door and through the knee-high grass between the parsonage and the meetinghouse. Rounding the corner of the stark building, she slowed and made herself calm down. There were the children, picking around the edge of the berry patch that had sprung up where the men had felled trees several years earlier. They were fine. They laughed together in the sunshine, and the smell of the leaves and the warm, plump berries encouraged her. She walked onward, swinging the kettle.

"Miss Christine!" Constance let out a squeal and ran to greet her.

"I thought I'd help you, and we'd finish picking sooner." Christine gently pulled up the bonnet Constance had let fall back on her shoulders. "You must shade yourself from the sun, dear."

Ben looked askance at her but kept picking without comment, and soon they had more than enough fruit for two pies.

"We could pick more and make jam," Abby suggested.

"Why not?" Christine also gathered blackberry leaves to dry for tea.

As they headed home at last, John and his father came ambling along the village street.

"Hello," the pastor called. "I see you are all out foraging."

"Aye, sir," said Christine. "You shall have fresh blackberry pie when you sit down to dinner."

"I look forward to it with pleasure." He handed her a small leather pouch. "Your share of the linen money."

"Oh. Thank you." Christine felt the blood rush to her cheeks. She tucked the pouch quickly away, in the pocket tied about her waist beneath her overskirt.

"Mrs. Heard was most pleased, and she says if you have time to make more, she'd be delighted to get it."

"My next project is already begun. Dark gray woolen for the boys' new trousers."

He nodded. "Well, I appreciate that, but I don't begrudge you to earn more if you can."

"Thank you."

Ben and John carried the bundles the pastor had purchased at the trading post, and the minister left them to enter the meetinghouse and study for his Sunday sermon.

Christine headed for home with the children. She wished she could unburden her heart to the pastor. But if she did, what evil would come to the family?

A sudden thought chilled her. The outlaw had demanded a blanket. But Goody Deane had no extra blankets, and surely if she took one from the parsonage it would be missed. All day she thought about it.

In the afternoon, she sorted through Elizabeth's clothes and selected an everyday linsey-woolsey skirt that she could make over for Abby. With care, she could probably make a dress for Ruth from the material, as well. Samuel had offered her his wife's Sunday skirt and bodice, but she had turned him down. It would not be so long before Abby was big enough to wear them.

As an afterthought, she examined the bed linens in the trunk kept in the loft. The family didn't need many blankets at present, and three quilts were neatly folded there. But she couldn't give one of those to the stranger. Elizabeth had stitched them with her own hands. Not only would the family need them in cold weather, but they would be heirlooms for the three girls. Beneath them, in the bottom of the chest, she found a tattered woolen blanket. That might do. Surely no one would miss it for months, and if she worked hard, she might be able to weave some thick, blanket-weight wool after the trousers and Pastor Jewett's new coat were finished, though those projects would take her the rest of the summer.

When she descended the ladder, Goody Deane picked up her basket. "I shall go over to my house now and lay supper on for the two of us, unless you plan to eat here tonight."

"I'll be there to dine with you," Christine said. She hated the thought of the old woman's possibly encountering the thief if she ventured about alone. "Would you like Master John to walk you home?"

"Me? Nay, I can take myself across the street."

Christine almost protested further but could see no logical reason to do so. She had never been overly solicitous of the old woman in such matters. After all, Tabitha had fended for herself for years. If Christine began to fuss over her, she would get suspicious. "Very well, but do let us know if you need help with anything."

While the children gathered the clean laundry off the clothesline behind the house, she managed to smuggle the old blanket outside and hide it in the woodpile, where she could get it when she left. And what would she take the man for sustenance? If she came with no food, he would no doubt rant at her. She wrapped two biscuits in a napkin and set them aside. She didn't like to take him anything that required dishes. Returning them would be too obvious. And the Jewetts were already watching their food supply since the disappearing-pie episode.

And so it was with only the biscuits and blanket that she headed out that night after dark. She told Goody Deane she would make a quick trip to the necessary. When she reached the edge of the woods, she waited for a minute in the spot where the man had accosted her the night before, but all was still. She laid the blanket down, with the biscuits on top. An animal might get the food. But if the blanket were gone in the morning, she would know he had come for it. And if it remained where she left it? She prayed it would. For then she could assume he had moved on.

&

After evening prayers on Thursday, the parishioners stood about the green in the balmy evening air. The Dudleys and others whose homes were a mile or two away set out, but those who lived close lingered. The hour after Thursday meeting was the social time of the week, more so than on Sunday as the people had more freedom on weekdays to laugh and jest. The talk this week reverted to the rash of purloining suffered by the villagers. Samuel Jewett stood to one side discussing with William Heard the work to be done on the meetinghouse, but he kept one ear tuned to the conversation behind him.

"I think it's just folks not paying attention and then blaming the imaginary thief," said Mr. Lyford, who owned the gristmill.

"Nay, not so," said Joseph Paine, the trader, who also served as the town's constable now. "There be too many reports of things missing."

"That's right." Daniel Otis, the blacksmith's son, stepped

forward. "I was smoothing the handle of a pitchfork I was making last week. I laid it by at milking time, with my knife beside it. When I came out of the byre and went to take it up again, my knife was missing. Clean gone. I looked all about and asked my family, but we've not found it yet. I'm afraid an Indian took it. With what designs, I won't speculate. We're locking up our tools, day and night, you can be sure."

"Young Stephen Dudley goes about as quiet as an Indian," Mahalia Ackley said.

Her husband smiled sheepishly. "Aye, he scares me. Came up behind me in my cornfield t'other day. I'd no idea the lad was about, and when he spoke to me, it startled me so I dropped my hoe on my foot."

The other men and their wives laughed.

"That Stephen's a sly one, that he is," said Lyford.

"It comes of his living with the savages all those years." Goody Ackley nodded emphatically. "I wonder if he's not the pilferer, I do."

Otis huffed out his breath. "What makes you say that? He's a good lad."

"But he's so stealthy. Them Indians taught him to skulk about, and no doubt he learned to steal, too." Goody Ackley glared at Otis, as though daring him to contradict her.

"Careful, ma'am," said Pastor Jewett, and all heads turned toward him. "Speaking ill of someone without a shred of evidence to support the accusation can bring you trouble."

"That's right," said the trader.

"I meant no ill," Mahalia Ackley said quickly. "I only said how furtivelike he moves. And it's the truth he stayed with those Indians long after he had a chance to go home to his folks. We all know his brother went to find him in Canada, and he wouldn't come back. He—"

"Enough." Samuel's steely voice silenced her. He advanced

a step toward the couple and looked into her eyes. "I tell you, madam, such talk does not become you."

Constable Paine took up a rigid stance beside the parson. "Indeed. This is gossip of the worst kind that can ruin a young man's reputation."

"Aye," said Otis. "If there is indeed a thief among us, Stephen Dudley be an unlikely candidate. Why would a young man whose father owns a thriving farm steal a knife? Why would a lad whose mother can outcook all the goodwives in Cochecho steal a few biscuits and a dish of sauerkraut?"

"Goody Ackley, desist from this train of conversation or you shall find yourself in the stocks tomorrow," Paine told her.

"Hmpf." Mahalia lifted her skirt and turned toward her husband. "Husband, I believe it is time we went home."

"A truer word was never spoken," William Heard muttered as the woman marched toward the street with her husband trailing behind her, his chin on his chest.

Paine clapped his hand to Samuel's shoulder. "Thank you for that, Parson."

Samuel shook his head. "I should have spoken to her privately first."

"Nay, she's let her tongue run too many times in public. You'd think she would learn after the times she's spent in the stocks."

Samuel couldn't help a pang of guilt. Paine represented the law, and he would have put the woman in her place without his own interference. As minister, he needed to stay neutral in local wranglings. Still, he'd felt a compulsion to stand up for Stephen and put a stop to Mahalia's vicious talk.

"Well, time to get my children home and into bed." He looked about for them and noticed Christine. She had the three girls and John clustered about her, waiting a short distance off. Ben had edged into the fringe of the knot of adults, but he detached himself and walked toward the family, reaching them just as Samuel did.

"Shall we be off?" Samuel asked Christine.

"Aye, sir."

They turned toward the parsonage in silence. When they reached the house, Christine entered without asking whether he wanted her presence and helped the girls prepare for bed. Samuel placed his Bible on the shelf and hung up his coat. When he turned, Ben and John were standing by the loom, watching him.

"To bed, boys."

"Father," Ben said, "people can't accuse Stephen of stealing like that, can they? He wouldn't do such a thing."

"Nay. There's no evidence of such a thing. Goody Ackley is a malicious gossip, that is all. No one puts store in what she says. I say that to you in private, however. It is not something I would wish you to say among others."

"Even if it's true?" John asked.

"There be times, John, when we ought to keep silence—especially young people. I perhaps should not have spoken out tonight. There were others present who could have done the job better than I, and as pastor, I must be particularly careful."

Ben nodded, but his face still held a troubled expression.

Samuel walked over to him and touched his arm. "Don't brood on it, son." He gave John a quick hug. "Good night, John."

The boys climbed the ladder to the loft just as Christine came from the girls' bedchamber.

"Thank you, Christine. Allow me to escort you home."

"There's no need."

"I don't like you to go about alone at night, especially with all this talk of thievery."

He thought her cheeks flushed, but in the poor candlelight he might be mistaken.

"Thank you, sir," she said softly. They walked across the way together.

"I hope Goody Deane feels better tomorrow," Samuel said. Christine had made the widow's excuses earlier, telling him she had a catarrh.

"She thought it best to stay away from the children for a few days, and I agreed. She'll be better off to stay home and rest than to come over to the parsonage and wear herself out with scrubbing and cooking when she's ill."

They reached the cottage door, and she paused. "Thank you, sir."

He looked down at her plain face in the moonlight. A year ago she would have averted her eyes in his presence and tried to avoid his notice at all cost. How far she had come in a year. She was still markedly reserved, but no vestige of fear remained. What a blessing she had been to his family.

"Christine, I appreciate all you've done for the children. For myself, as well."

After a moment, she looked away. "I enjoy doing for your family."

He nodded. "I thank God for you every day. Good night now."

She put her hand to the latch, and he turned away.

ﺰ

Christine stood inside the little cottage, her back to the door, listening. Goody Deane's labored breathing broke the stillness. The poor woman's nose was clogged, no doubt, which made her snoring more pronounced.

Christine had not encountered the outlaw tonight. Perhaps that was due to Pastor Jewett's presence. If she stayed with other people and didn't give him the opportunity to catch her alone, perhaps she could avoid ever talking to him again.

Or maybe he had left the area. She didn't really believe that, with all the reports in the village. And if he left Cochecho, he would work his evil somewhere else. Did she really want him to go about threatening other people and stealing from them?

The old blanket she'd left at the edge of the woods had disappeared. He had at least taken that last night.

She walked to the kitchen window and pushed the muslin curtain aside. A bank of clouds obscured the moon, and she thought it likely to rain before morning. The wind stirred the branches.

Was he out there, even now, watching the cottage? She shivered and turned away.

five

Friday was the scheduled workday at the meetinghouse, and Samuel planned carefully so that he could spend the day with the men of the parish, who would give of their time to make improvements on the building.

For years the church folk had talked about building better pews inside—enclosed seating for each family, rather than the rows of plain benches they now used. Constructing a fireplace at one side of the building had also been bandied about, with the conclusion that they could get along as they always had in winter—with their foot warmers and soapstones and hot bricks wrapped in sacking. Some members even brought their dogs to church in winter and persuaded the animals to lie on their feet and keep them warm, but this sometimes resulted in disruption of the service.

Samuel had tried not to take sides in the debate, though in his mind a fireplace would have done them all good. As it was, they retired to nearby houses at noon to get warm on winter Sundays, returning to the frigid meetinghouse for the second sermon. Of course, attempting to heat such a large, open building would take a lot of fuel, which meant the men would have to give more labor toward providing wood. As it was, the parsonage sometimes went short of fuel in winter. He didn't like to ask them to do more, especially as the nearby supply of firewood was dwindling and the settlers went farther each year to furnish their woodpiles.

But the pews were another thing. The elders had agreed that the boxlike pews with four-foot partition walls were what they needed. These would give each family privacy and prevent the churchgoers from the distraction of eyeing their neighbors during the service. These enclosures would be built around the edge of the room, and William Heard's plan allowed for six more in the middle. The pulpit would be raised on a small platform, enabling all the people to see the minister while they were seated.

James Dudley arrived early, while the grass was still wet from the rain, with his cart loaded with lumber. Samuel heard the cart creaking up the street and called to Ben and John to join him. James and his son Stephen walked beside the cart, and Samuel hurried to help them unload.

"My brother and Charles Gardner be coming, too," Stephen told the pastor. "Richard and Charles are carrying the babies, so that the ladies can take them to visit at the parsonage today."

"Splendid," Samuel said. He looked back down the street and saw the two young men, their wives, the elder Mrs. Dudley, and her eighteen-year-old daughter, Catherine, approaching along the track that led to their outlying farms. "The ladies will have a good day together, and I'm sure they'll put on a toothsome luncheon for us."

William Heard and two of his sons arrived next, bearing tools and a small keg of sweet cider. "Richard Otis be bringing plenty of nails," Heard reported. On top of the stack of wide boards, he unrolled the plan he had drawn to guide them in their work.

"Do you plan to have a boys' pew?" James Dudley looked over Heard's shoulder at the meticulous diagram.

Heard glanced at Samuel. "What say ye, pastor? Methinks we decided not."

"That's right, Brother William. I know they do it some places, but in my opinion, boys will behave better if they sit with their own families. Let the fathers keep them in line."

Heard nodded. "So be it. The deacons will have their places here, and the pews we have planned will accommodate all of the regular parishioners and visitors, with room for a few new families."

"Aye, our village is growing." Samuel made a mental note to visit a new family that had taken up residence within the township, upriver toward the falls. "But we shall leave it to the deacons to assign the pews."

He could picture his five children, with Christine Hardin and Tabitha Deane, of course, in the front, center pew, sitting straight and listening attentively as he spoke. What would he have done without those two ladies this past year? The thought of Christine moving to another family's pew— whether as a maid to one of the church ladies or as the wife of another man—disturbed him. He shook off the thought and picked up his hammer.

❧

At the parsonage, the women gathered with great joy. A day together was a treat for all, though they would spend it working hard. Christine especially enjoyed cuddling her friends' babies and helping Constance and Abigail take turns holding the little ones.

"You shall have to come out to the farm again soon, Christine," Jane Gardner said. "Charles has finally finished my loom, and I wish you would help me to warp it the first time."

"I'd love to."

"Good," said Sarah Dudley. "Richard says the sheep have grown their wool back prodigious-fast, and he plans to shear them again next week. We'll have an abundance of wool this year."

Goody Dudley set a heavy basket on the table. "I brought

extra dishes, and I'd like to leave a few here for the pastor. You have church folk to feed fairly often, Christine, and with all the children. . .well, I thought giving the parson a few extra plates would not be amiss, and I put in a couple of tin cups the children can use."

"Bless you," Christine said. "Those will be most welcome."

She directed her guests in preparing a huge pot of bean soup and another of mutton stew for the workmen. Goody Dudley and Catherine had brought the ingredients for a prune pudding, and they started it cooking. As the morning waned, Goody Deane offered to bake a batch of biscuits on her own hearth across the street, and Goody Dudley went with her. The younger women contributed to the preparation of another batch of biscuits and a large pan of corn bread at the parsonage.

While Jane's baby boy napped, Abby and Constance played with Hannah Dudley and Ruth.

With the little ones out of earshot, Jane turned the talk to a more sensitive matter. "You know the Wales wedding is Sunday."

"Aye." Christine shaped the biscuits with a round cutter and laid them in the Dutch oven. "Pastor Jewett is performing the rites at noon. If the weather is fine, we're to take food and eat in the churchyard. Parthenia's family is providing cake for everyone afterward."

"It will be strange to call her Goody Wales," Catherine said. "But since Goodman Jones died, I suppose she is taking the best course for herself and her children."

"I don't know about that," said Jane. "The second Mrs. Wales didn't live long after she married him. Only five years or so."

Sarah shrugged. "And the first one less than ten. Are you saying the Wales women are short-lived?"

"If I were her, I'd be cautious," Jane said.

Sarah chuckled. "Really, Jane, you're so droll."

Jane, who had experienced an unhappy marriage and widowhood, shrugged and went on with her task of measuring the ground corn. Christine felt that Jane took the matter more seriously than Sarah did but saw no profit in pursuing the topic.

The urge to tell them about the threatening stranger rose in Christine's mind, but she checked the impulse. What good would telling them do? And she had heard nothing from him in two days, nor any fresh stories of thievery. Better to forget it and let others forget it, too.

"I'm giving Parthenia a set of two linen towels," she said.

"I'm embroidering an apron for her." Catherine cracked two eggs into her mixing bowl while Sarah greased a large pan for her.

The baby began to cry, and Jane hurried to fetch him.

"So, Christine," Catherine said as she stirred the batter for the corn pone, "I heard Goody Ackley asked you to work for her."

"I declined."

"Which was probably your best choice," Catherine admitted, "though I'd love to have you closer. If you were at the Ackleys' farm, I'd doubtless get to see you more often."

"I would like that, too," Christine said, "but I am happy with my position here. I've grown to love the children dearly, and I think the Jewetts really need me." She felt her face flushing and feared the others would misconstrue her words. "That is, they need *someone*, and. . .well, the Lord put me here."

"That's right." Sarah smiled at her. "The Lord put all of us here two years ago—you, Jane, and me. I know you're a blessing to Pastor Jewett and his family."

Jane's eyes twinkled as she returned with little John Gardner held against her shoulder. "So perhaps you'll be best off to stay here, as Sarah and I did, until the Lord brings along a husband for you."

"Oh nay," Christine returned with a laugh. "No husband for me. I'm content in the state I'm in. My employer may not be so well fixed as Goodman Ackley, but I believe the atmosphere here to be more congenial."

"You speak truth," said Jane.

The day flew by. When the ladies had served dinner to the men and cleaned up the remaining food and dishes, they sat down at the parsonage to do their handwork, whether knitting, mending, or stitchery. All too soon, the Dudley men returned to take their womenfolk home. Goody Deane went to her own cottage while Christine prepared supper for the Jewett family. It was short work, with all the food left from the nooning.

Christine stayed until sunset, straightening up the main room while John and Abby did the dishes.

When they had finished, she carried the pan of dirty dishwater around to the garden behind the house. With the hot, dry weather, the vegetable plants could use every drop of moisture the household could give them. She sloshed the water out along a row of parsnips and was about to return to the house, when a tall, thin man appeared between the shoulder-high cornstalks.

She gasped and stared at him, knowing at once that he was the outlaw. She had never seen him in good light before, but his lean form, unkempt beard, and ragged clothing left no doubt.

"You've not brung me anything these two nights." He stayed within the line of the nearest corn row, and his eyes flickered toward the house.

She swallowed with difficulty. "I thought you'd gone."

"Nay."

"You've been eating, though." She looked into his flinty gray eyes.

His lips twitched. "Aye, short shrift it's been. But you've cooked a great heap of food today. I saw the men eating in the churchyard. I says to myself, 'You'll eat tonight, you will.' Bring me a plate. I'll wait here."

"I can't fix a plate and carry it out now that the family is done eating. Everyone would want to know what it was for."

"Tell them it's for the widow."

Christine's heart clenched. He knew so much about them. She could probably do that, and the Jewetts would accept her word. But she wouldn't lie to them. How could she ever look into the reverend's kind brown eyes knowing she'd lied to him?

"Nay."

His eyes narrowed. "Be you forgettin' what I said? You'd best bring me a plate, out back of the widow's house, at full dark."

"I won't."

He looked toward the house again. "Then I'll get it myself and not care who I slash to get it."

"No. You mustn't." She gripped the tin basin tightly. "I'll. . . I'll bring you something."

"Good. And I need a pair of trousers."

Christine felt as though the breath had been pummeled out of her. "How do you expect me to come by those?"

"The parson. I can fit his togs."

"Nay. He is a poor man. You can't steal his clothing."

"Would you have me go about indecent? 'Twill soon come to that."

Involuntarily, she glanced down at his ragged trousers. Both knees were torn through and a large tear gaped in the side of one pant leg.

"Can't you get them elsewhere?"

"I've tried, but I have to be careful, you know."

She gritted her teeth. "Oh yes, I know. You're such an honest man you must stay hidden from all the law-abiding people hereabouts."

His expression darkened. "Enough. Bring me food, and plenty of it, and a pair of trousers with no rips." He disappeared into the cornfield.

six

Christine returned to the parsonage with a heavy heart. It was true, the man's clothing was in tatters from his weeks of skulking about. A small part of her felt sorry for him. But his gruesome threats hardened even the most tender spots in her heart.

I should have told Samuel!

The thought shocked her, because she never thought of the Reverend Mr. Jewett as Samuel. He was Pastor, or Mr. Jewett. But he was also her friend, and now his family was in danger. If she followed her impulse to tell Samuel about the outlaw, what would he do? At once she knew he would organize a search for the criminal. But what if the man were crafty enough to elude them? He'd gone uncaught for some time now. She didn't know where he was getting his food on nights when he didn't demand it from her. Perhaps other women in the village were as frightened as she was and handing over rations to him, too.

He has to be stopped, Lord!

Her prayer seemed futile. If she revealed the man's demands, he would know it, and he would do something horrible to the pastor's children.

Stealthily she took the pastor's workday trousers from the clothespress. He had two other pairs, his best for Sunday, and the pair he wore most days, when going about the parish to visit his flock. She ran a finger over the neat patch on one knee of the oldest pair. His dear, dead wife had stitched that patch on with love.

Forgive me, Father. I don't know what else I can do. I must protect the children. If there is a better way, then show me.

ào

He was waiting when she took the food and folded trousers out that night. She sensed his presence before she saw him. Was it an odor, or an influence of evil?

"What took you so long?"

"I had to make sure Goody Deane was asleep."

He snatched the bundle. "I like to have perished waiting."

"Please, I don't know how I'm going to explain to the parson about his trousers."

"You'll think of something. Just remind yourself that if I get to looking decent, I can show myself and look for work. You're helping me become an honest man, that you are. I do want to be honest."

She wanted to believe him, but his manner and his past actions prevented that. She had managed to get out of the parsonage undetected with a covered dish of stew. He pulled the linen napkin off and dropped it on the ground, then he tipped the bowl up to his mouth.

"I brought you a spoon."

He lowered the dish, wiped his lips with the back of his hand, and reached for it.

Christine shuddered as she put the spoon in his hand.

"Why ain't you got a husband?"

She stiffened. "I beg your pardon?"

"You heard me." He took a bite of stew and kept talking as he chewed. "It's true you're homely, but you seem a fair cook and a hard worker. That counts for a lot."

She stared at him for a moment, scarcely able to believe he had spoken to her in that manner. "Put the dishes on the window ledge when you are finished." She turned and stalked into the house.

৯

After the eventful weekend, Samuel needed a rest. All of Friday and a good part of Saturday he had spent helping William Heard and the other men build the new pews. Samuel left off on Saturday afternoon to put in more time on his sermon preparations.

The men had finished the work inside the church by Saturday night. The next morning, the parishioners seemed suitably impressed by the accomplishment. Elder Sawyer had assigned the pews. Of course there were a few minor squabbles over which family should have which box, but Samuel left that entirely to the elders. Roger and Mahalia Ackley tried to corner him to complain about their pew's position after the service, but he quickly excused himself, since he had to prepare for the marriage ceremony.

After the morning's sermon, he performed the marriage rite for Mordecai Wales and Parthenia Jones. This was followed by the usual nooning hour and then the afternoon service, which lasted three hours.

By sunset on Sunday, Samuel was always wrung out. Christine had prepared a cold supper for him and the children Sunday night and then left them to a quiet evening and early retirement. He slept through the night, hardly stirring from the moment his head hit the feather pillow.

But now Monday had dawned, and he longed to stretch his muscles and do some physical labor. He climbed out of bed, knelt to pray for his family and congregation, then arose and went to the pine chest where he kept his clothing.

His shirts, all but the one he'd worn yesterday, were folded neatly inside. His Sunday breeches and second-best pair likewise. His stockings and drawers occupied a corner. But his workaday trousers—the ones he wore when gardening or helping one of the farmers with haying—were nowhere to be found. He looked around the room in confusion then put on his second-best breeches, his oldest, most worn shirt, lightweight stockings, a leather waistcoat, and shoes. Then he emerged into the great room.

Christine had already arrived, and she knelt by the hearth to kindle a cooking fire.

"Christine."

"Yes, sir?" She swiveled on her heels to look at him.

"Where are my old trousers?"

She hesitated a moment, and her face colored.

Of course, under ordinary circumstances it would be considered vulgar for a man to mention his trousers in the presence of an unmarried female. But after all, Christine did his mending and laundry. Indeed, she had sewn some of his clothing, and she handled his most intimate garments almost daily. They ought to be able to discuss them.

"I am stitching a new pair for you, sir." She ducked her head and seemed inordinately concerned with coaxing her pile of tinder to catch a flame.

Samuel cocked his head to one side and considered that. "Did you take the old ones to use as a pattern?"

After a long moment, she said without turning around, "I might have."

"Ah. Then I suppose I must garden in such as I wear now. Permit me to tend the fire for you."

"It's going now. But if you'd care to bring in more water, I won't say nay. This be my washing day."

"Of course."

Samuel picked up the two water buckets and emptied them into the largest kettle he owned. As he walked the short distance to the river for more water, he went over the brief conversation in his mind. It didn't make much sense to him, but he was certain Christine had a purpose. His old trousers weren't that bad, but they did bear a couple of patches. Neat patches, it was true, but perhaps she felt it an embarrassment to have the minister go about in patched trousers. Still, he wouldn't wear the old ones if he were going around the village.

He gave it up and raised a quiet prayer as he dipped the buckets full of water. "Thank You, Lord, for trousers, and for shirts and shoes and hose. Thank You for Christine and the labor she bestows so willingly on our family."

Yes, Christine was a blessing to be thankful for. She would make some man a fine wife, if only she were willing to marry. Of course, if she did, he and the children would be lost without her. What a pity for Christine to live a solitary life, never knowing the joys of marriage.

The sweet companionship of his wife, Elizabeth, had carried him through many a painful situation. He missed her terribly. She'd been gone more than a year now; again the idea flitted through his mind that perhaps it was time to consider marrying again. This was not the first time the concept had occurred to him, but still the thought stabbed him with a dagger of guilt. And yet, scripture allowed it.

"Ah, Lord, Thou hast said it is not good for man to be alone. Yet whenever I think of replacing my dear Elizabeth, it pains me so much I cannot contemplate it."

The sun beat already on his shoulders, foretelling another sweltering August day. He reached his doorstep and went inside. Ruth and the boys were up, and Christine had them seated at the table eating corn pone and bacon.

He glanced toward the loom and saw that her new weaving was of fine charcoal gray worsted, a mixture of fine linen thread and wool. For him and the boys. She wouldn't be able to sell it if she used it on clothing for them, and he would have nothing to pay her this month. She didn't seem to mind.

She met his gaze, and he noted a slight apprehension in her hazel eyes.

He smiled as he set the buckets down. "I neglected to say good morning, Christine. Forgive me."

Her expression cleared.

"And good day to you, sir. Will you break your fast now?"

⁂

After breakfast was over, Ruth was changed out of her night-clothes, the hearth swept, and the dishes cleaned, Christine began her washing. Ben carried the kettle of hot water out behind the house and emptied it into the washtub. He and John brought several buckets of cold water to add to it, and she wound up with a lukewarm bath for the family's clothing and linens.

Constance and Abby helped her. After Christine had scrubbed a garment on the washboard, she tossed it into the tub of rinse water. The girls' job was to retrieve it, dunk it in a bucket that held a second rinse water, wring it again, and hang it on the clothesline. She kept the two little girls busy running back and forth. Constance couldn't reach the line, but she handed the wet clothes to Abby, who was a head taller and proud that she could perform this task.

Meanwhile, the pastor and his sons weeded the garden and picked the vegetables that were ripe. The peas were gone by, but beets, lettuce, Swiss chard, green beans, carrots, turnips, and onions would liven up their meals. Last year's root vegetables were nearly exhausted, and what was left had gone soft. The new harvest cheered everyone.

Christine attacked the pile of soiled clothing with a vengeance. She had brought her own and Goody Deane's laundry over, to save time and resources. If she finished this daunting task by noon, she would do the ironing after dinner and perhaps snatch a couple of hours at the loom.

Such a shame that the reverend had discovered the loss of his old trousers so quickly. She should have expected it on a Monday, she supposed. Samuel often took that day to catch up on chores around the parsonage. The worsted suit she now intended to sew for him would be suitable for Sunday best, however. It wouldn't actually replace his work clothes. He could wear the older breeches, as he did today, but she knew he preferred his comfortable long trousers for dirty work.

As she scrubbed, she racked her brain for a way to get him some serviceable trousers. Perhaps Jane or Sarah could help her, but if she asked them, she might have to reveal what she had done with the old pair. And making Samuel an entire new suit would delay weaving the thicker wool cloth she needed to make him a new winter coat.

She sighed and wrung out Ruth's nightdress, the last of the light-colored clothes. Stooping, she lifted an armful of darker clothing into the washtub. As she straightened, she looked out over the garden and corn patch. Was the outlaw watching them, even now, from the edge of the forest?

He had come the past three nights, and she had taken him small amounts of food. It had become her routine. They met in darkness, while Goody Deane slumbered. Once the old woman had woken in her absence, and Christine had dodged her questions, feeling guilty. Each time she met the outlaw, he told her that he wanted to do honest work. Yet he continued to intimidate her into feeding him.

Where was Ruth? A sudden panic seized Christine, and she whirled about. Ah. There she was, playing with her dolly, Lucy, near the woodpile.

"Abby, bring Ruth closer, where I can watch her. She can sit in the shade of the rose bush." Christine looked once more toward the line of trees beyond the cornfield. Perhaps it was her imagination, but she felt him watching.

seven

Christine asked Ben to escort her and his three sisters to the Gardners' farm on Tuesday. Leaving them there with Jane, he went to spend the day working with Richard Dudley and Charles Gardner, who were gathering hay from Charles's field, within sight of the house.

"What's that you're working on?" Jane asked as Christine pulled a roll of linsey-woolsey from her workbag.

"It's material Goody Dudley gave me last spring. I was hoping there would be enough to make some everyday trousers for the reverend, but I fear there's not."

"He needs clothes?"

Christine hesitated. "Well, I'm weaving some nice worsted for a new Sunday winter suit for him, but he really needs something to work about the place without fear of ruining it."

"Ah. Well, I might have something."

"Your Charles is taller than the pastor."

"This is none of his clothing."

"Well, don't give me anything you and Charles will need."

"Nay, 'tis a piece of cloth he picked up for me on his trip to Boston last month. He brought home a bolt of serge, for which I was grateful, and two pieces of flannel for the baby, and a bit of blue silk." Jane smiled, her cheeks going a becoming pink. "He said I should make myself a bodice from the silk, but I don't know as I'd dare wear it. The women of Cochecho would think I was putting on airs."

"I think it would be lovely, and it would please Charles."

"Perhaps. Anyway, there's this piece of coarse cotton. He said he thought I might use it for pillow ticking, but it's not near so fine as I'd like in a pillow." Jane went into the next room and returned with a folded length of cloth.

Christine ran her hand over it. "That would do. If you're certain. . ."

"Oh, I am."

Christine nodded. "I'll spin for you in exchange."

"Nonsense."

"Nay, you do far too much for me."

The baby cried, and Jane smiled. "There's Johnny, awake from his nap. After I feed him, I'll help you cut out the pieces."

Christine went out to check on the little girls. They played inside the fence that surrounded the house, barn, woodshed, and yard.

"We're building a house for the dollies." Constance took her hand and led her to where they had formed a little stick house from twigs they'd gathered in the yard.

"Goodman Gardner has a baby calf yonder. And we got to pet it." Abby pointed to the small barn. "Do you want to see it?"

Christine caught a glimpse of color through a slit between the upright posts of the palisade. "I should love to, but I see young Mrs. Dudley coming along the path. Shall we go meet her? We can help her carry some of baby Hannah's things, perhaps."

"I'm so glad to see you," Sarah called as they approached. "Richard doesn't like me to walk even this far alone, but I could see him and Charles working almost as soon as I left my own doorstep, so I knew he wouldn't mind." She handed a basket to Abby and a small sack to Constance. "Thank you, my dears. Hannah is eager to play with you."

Sarah provided not only a store of anecdotes to entertain them but a pudding for the dinner she and Richard would share with the Gardners and their guests. Jane and Sarah set about preparing the noon meal while Christine took out her mending, and the little girls settled to play with Hannah and John on a blanket on the floor.

"Richard's mother paid a call on Goody Ackley yesterday." Sarah chopped scallions while Jane punched down her bread dough and set it to rise a second time. "Mahalia had asked her if she had any rye flour left, so Mother Dudley took over a small sack. She found Alice Stevens rather put upon."

"Oh?" said Jane. "Isn't that a maid's lot?"

"Aye. But Mother thought Mahalia treated her ill. Whatever the girl did, the goodwife complained in front of Mother until Alice was so nervous she dropped the plate of biscuits she was serving."

"Oh, dear."

"What did she do?" Christine asked.

"Mahalia screamed at her and told her to go and finish the washing. Mother Dudley said Alice was crying when she left the house."

"It's too bad." Christine knotted her thread and broke it off.

"Aye," Sarah said. "Alice was always a pretty and pleasant girl, if a bit timid. I fear she'll turn into a cowering ninny if she stays long at the Ackleys'. After she went out, her mistress told Mother Dudley she was a sly, sniveling girl and not nearly so good at cleaning as the last one."

"Well, I'm glad it's not me." Christine took out one of Ben's socks and her darning egg.

"You did well not to go there." Sarah wiped her hands on her apron and sat down on a bench. From her basket, she took a hank of soft lavender woolen yarn.

"Oh, how lovely," Christine said.

"How did you ever get it that color?" Jane came around the table to peer at it more closely.

"Mother Dudley did it. She's a clever one. Boiled it with the paper that came wrapped around a sugar cone. Isn't it the prettiest color? I thought to knit a wrap for Hannah to wear when the cooler weather sets in."

"She'll look darling in it." Jane set her bread pans on a shelf. "Come, Christine, let's lay out that cotton and cut it. We've time before dinner."

As they walked home later, Ben carried his littlest sister, Ruth, on his shoulders, and Constance held tight to Christine's hand. Abby walked alongside, carrying her diminutive basket with her rag doll and sampler tucked inside.

Christine let her thoughts wander to the late afternoon conversation she and Jane had held, after Sarah left them.

"How do you know you can trust a man?" It was the closest she dared come to asking Jane's opinion about the outlaw. But Jane had jumped to the wrong conclusion.

"Who is he?" Her face had lit with excitement. "Christine, don't tell me that at last you're in love!"

"No! Not that. I was only asking. You know I've never lived around men much."

"Until the reverend."

"Well. . .yes, but I wasn't thinking of him. Truly."

"Ah." Jane turned sober then, bouncing the baby on her lap. "Well then, I suppose you must spend time with him and talk to him, until you feel you know him quite well."

Christine wanted to protest. Spending time with the shadowy thief was the last thing she would do. But looking across the room at the three little girls playing so placidly with Hannah, she knew she couldn't reveal the truth. No palisade surrounded the parsonage in Cochecho. Samuel Jewett had bought a musket only when he felt it absolutely necessary because of the frequent Indian raids. If the outlaw struck at his children, he would be hard pressed to protect them. Let Jane think what she may, Christine must keep her secret.

And so she left embarrassed and confused. Jane had automatically assumed that her affections were set on the minister. Given the circumstances, the entire village probably thought as much. But Samuel. . . Christine shifted the heavy basket on her arm. What *were* her feelings for Samuel?

❧

Two nights later, by sitting up and sewing by candlelight, Christine finished making the new work trousers for the pastor. She put the last stitch in the hem late. As she stood and folded them, every muscle ached. Somehow she had to rid herself of this anxiety.

Her prayers seemed to have become vain repetitions—*Father, show me what to do. Lord, keep the children safe.* Mindlessly, she went about her daily work to make them comfortable. And every night she took their potential assailant sustenance so he could come back again tomorrow and threaten them again.

Something thunked against the side of the house, just below the window. She blew out the candle and stood in the dark, her heart racing.

Plink.

It sounded like a pebble had hit the boards outside. He had returned. He expected her to bring him food, and she hadn't gone out yet tonight. If she didn't go, he would keep up the racket, possibly awakening Tabitha.

With shaking hands, she carried the candle to the fireplace and relit it from the dying embers. She hastened to gather a scanty meal for him. There wasn't much, but she had deliberately put aside a small portion of dried fish, not admitting to herself at the time that it was for the lurker. And she had left half of her Indian pudding uneaten to sneak it into a covered dish when Tabitha looked the other way.

Another pebble hit the side of the house as she lifted the latch. Carefully balancing the earthenware dish, she slipped outside and closed the door behind her.

"Thought you'd forgotten me."

She jumped, almost dropping the dish. "Hush! You mustn't come so near the house."

He edged away, into the herb garden.

She still held the dish, and so she followed.

He went to the shadows beneath a large maple and turned toward her. "Well, lass, bring it here."

She hesitated. Why had she even bothered to ask Jane about trust? She didn't trust this miscreant one whit. "Nay. I'll leave it here." She stooped to set the dish on the ground.

"What, afraid of me?"

"Should I not be?"

"I'll not hurt ye, Christine."

She shuddered. He had never used her name before. Had he asked someone in the village the name of the young woman who worked at the parsonage? More likely he'd heard the children call out to her weeks ago. Or perhaps he'd heard Goody Deane use her name the night she called out when she'd heard his voice. Christine couldn't remember, but it disturbed her that he acted so familiar.

"Leave us alone." She swallowed, hoping she could keep her voice steady. "This be the last time I will bring you anything."

"What? Ye cannot let me starve."

"Oh, but you can make us all live in fear."

He laughed. "I don't see anyone acting fearful. Anyone but you, that is."

Her anger simmered. In the darkness she thought he smiled. "You say you'll stop stealing, but you don't. I've given you food and clothing and a blanket that were not mine to give. You've made me steal for you. Do you hear me? You've made a thief of me. This must stop."

"Can you help me stop?"

"How would I do that?" she asked. He was toying with her, she thought, keeping her here in the shadows for his own purposes.

"You could speak for me to one of the gentlemen of the village. Tell them to hire me."

"Whom could you work for?"

"Anyone."

"The master at the brickyard?"

"Perhaps, though it's sorry work."

"Have you sought to hire on with the fishing captains?"

He flexed his shoulders. "Seasick, I fear. Debilitating."

She nodded. He would make excuses for any real job possibility, she calculated. "Harvest will soon be upon us. I know farmers who could use a hand at haying and grain harvest. Shall I speak to them for you?"

His momentary silence confirmed her assessment. He didn't want to work. Not really. At least, not hard, sweat-inducing, energy-sapping work.

"Certainly. But I shall need decent shoes and more food than you've been bringing me if I'm to slave all day in the sun."

"You new employer can feed and clothe you. I'll spread the word tomorrow. What is your name? How shall they find you?"

"Well, I. . ."

Again his hesitation emboldened her. She stepped toward him. "Speak, sir. Shall I put it about the village that a strong laborer will go to the ordinary at noon seeking employment?"

"Ye're a bit hasty, miss. I've not eaten well for many a week. I've not the strength you seem to think I have."

"Oh, haven't you? I've been kind to you. You know I have. Leave us. Just leave us. I won't tell anyone you were here."

"Nay, I think not." He stepped forward, and his face became clearer in the moonlight.

"I tell you now, sir, I cannot provide for you any longer."

He moved swiftly, another step forward. Suddenly they were toe-to-toe, with a glinting knife blade between them.

"You'll do as I say," he spat out in a low, raspy tone. "If you don't, you'll be nursing one of those little dark-haired girls tomorrow. See if one of them don't meet with an accident."

"Christine?" Goody Deane's sharp voice startled them both.

The man glanced toward the house, over Christine's shoulder, and melted back into the shadows beneath the tree.

Christine drew in a ragged breath and turned around. "I'm coming, Tabitha."

"Who was that man?" The widow peered toward the garden. "Shall I run for the parson?"

Christine reached her side. "Nay. He is. . ." She struggled to pull breath in past the heavy weight on her chest. "Oh, Tabitha, you cannot tell Reverend Jewett."

Goody Deane's eyes glittered as she frowned up at Christine. "What are you saying, girl? You've formed an attachment you're ashamed of."

"Nay. Oh please, don't think that!" Christine let out her breath and reached for Tabitha's hand. "I see I must tell you all."

"And about time, I'd say. Come inside. I'll stir up the fire, and we shall have blackberry tea and a bit of that Indian pudding you put by."

Christine stared at her. "You saw that?"

"Of course I did. You think I don't notice what goes on at my own hearth?"

Glancing behind her, Christine realized that the outlaw

had managed to grab the dish of food as he retreated. "Then you'll soon realize we won't be eating any pudding. And we may be out one dish as well, if he doesn't return it. But I expect I'll find it on the window ledge at dawn." Tears streamed down her cheeks, and she felt the absurd urge to laugh. "I'm relieved, actually, that you know.".

Tabitha squinted toward the dark expanse of the garden. A breeze ruffled the maple tree's leaves. "Come inside, my dear. I think this is a night to bar the door and bare your soul to God and a human friend."

eight

Samuel set four math problems for John on his slate Wednesday morning and immersed himself in the scripture for the Thursday evening sermon. So many distractions in summer. Ben was off working for James Dudley today, and John fidgeted. Every sound that reached them through the oiled paper window of the meetinghouse called to the ten-year-old boy. The oppressive heat found them, even inside the big building, though it was cooler inside than out in the scalding sun. It was a wonder the boy learned anything at all.

He thought of Christine and the girls, no doubt baking today, poor things. He'd told Christine she needn't build the fire this morning, but she insisted that if she didn't, they'd have no bread tomorrow and their fish would be presented raw at supper. He would keep himself and John away from the house all day so that she and the girls could work in their shifts. Even so, they were likely to swelter in the little house. Did they have plenty of water for their cooking and washing needs?

It took determination to put his household out of his mind. He had only another thirty hours before evening worship, and he had much work to do on Sunday's two sermons as well.

"Father."

Samuel looked up.

John stood beside him with his slate ready.

"Ah. Finished your problems, have you?"

"Aye."

"Good lad. Let me check them." He took the slate from his son and put his mind to work on the arithmetic. "Excellent. Now, study your Latin."

"Father, be we going home for dinner soon?"

"I told Miss Christine she could send Abby over with a cold luncheon for us. I don't wish to add to her work in this heat."

John nodded and wiped his brow with a kerchief. They had both stripped off their jackets and vests hours since, but even so, the back of Samuel's linen shirt stuck to his skin.

"May I get a drink now, Father?"

"Aye. Let us both." Samuel stood and set his Bible on the pew next to his ink bottle, quill pen, and two sheets of thin birch bark on which he'd been jotting notes for the sermon. Parchment was too expensive, and his scant supply of locally made paper was nearly gone. Perhaps he could replenish it when he received his quarterly salary, though many other needs seemed more pressing.

The door of the meetinghouse flew open, and Roger Ackley stood blinking in the doorway, panting for breath. He held his shabby coat in one hand, and his clay pipe was stuck in the band of his shapeless hat of beaver felt. "Reverend?"

"Aye, Brother Roger. How may I help you?" Samuel walked down the aisle between the new box pews.

"Ah, there ye be." Ackley stepped inside. "It's cool in here."

"Is it?" Samuel asked.

"Sir, I've come about my wife. Goody Ackley left for the trader this morning. She said she wished to go while the air was still bearable. She ought to have been back by half past nine, but she weren't. I sent Alice, the girl what be our maid now, to see if she were coming, but Alice didn't meet her. She went all the way to the trading post, and Paine said she came in early, just as she planned." He pulled in a deep breath and shook his head. "But it's past noon now, sir, and she never came back. I'm on my way to see Paine, and I thought you might be of help."

Samuel laid his hand on the older man's sleeve. "I'm sorry, Roger. We'll find her, I'm sure. I'll send word around the village. Perhaps she decided to visit one of the other women while she was in town."

"Perchance you're right, Parson, and I wouldn't fret most days, but you know we've had Indian trouble already this summer. This time of year, they come down out of Canada and worry us. You were there, sir, when they came at us after meeting last month, and Richard Otis was shot before we ran them off."

"Yes, I understand." Samuel turned to look at his son. "John, get Goodman Ackley a dipper of water. Then I want you to run home and tell Christine—oh, never mind! Here's Christine with our dinner. I'll tell her myself. Then we'll walk over to the trading post and speak to Mr. Paine."

"Can I go?" John asked eagerly. He scooped water out of the bucket near the door and handed the dripping dipper to Goodman Ackley.

"Aye, I'll let you go along, but you must stay with me." Samuel smiled at Christine as she mounted the steps, and he took the basket from her. He lifted the corner of the linen napkin to peek inside. "Thank you, Christine. That looks delicious. Are you suffering from the heat?"

"Prodigiously, sir."

He chuckled. "Well, we're thankful for the repast."

"I thought to speak to you, sir, if you've a moment."

Samuel wondered what her errand was. Probably something about household affairs. He stepped to one side, so she could see that he was not alone. "I'm afraid John and I must go straightway to the trading post to speak to Mr. Paine.

And I want you to keep the little girls close. Mrs. Ackley is missing, and until we find her, I want to know you are all safe at home."

Christine's hazel eyes widened, but she nodded without comment.

"Is Goody Deane with you at my house?"

"Yes, sir."

"That is well. Go now. I'll watch to be sure you get home safe."

He handed the basket of lunch to John and stood on the step until he saw Christine enter the parsonage next door.

"Here, Father. Biscuits, cheese, and baked fish."

"Ah. Loaves and fishes, as Christ gave to the five thousand. We must give extra thanks for the cheese." Samuel smiled. "Have you eaten, Brother Roger?"

"Nay."

"Then you must share what we have. Let us ask God's blessing, and we shall eat as we go, for I know your wife's well-being lies heavy on your heart just now and we must not delay."

"What is your plan, sir?" Ackley asked.

"Constable Paine first. I expect he'll start an organized inquiry throughout the town."

"And if we do not find her?"

"Why, then I suppose we must search elsewhere. But let us not borrow trouble."

❧

As men arrived on the common before the meetinghouse, Christine stood in the parsonage doorway and watched.

Joseph Paine had taken charge. He assigned each new cluster of arrivals an area to canvass.

"Surely they'll find she stopped to have dinner at a friend's house," Christine said.

Tabitha sat in the late Goody Jewett's chair, playing cat's cradle with Constance. "I don't know about that. Would you invite her to stay for a meal if she came by your house?"

Christine gritted her teeth together. She couldn't deny the truth—not many women in Cochecho liked Mahalia Ackley. Her venomous gossip had long since put her on the outs with all of her neighbors. Even the most tolerant ladies of the church avoided her. "Mayhap she felt ill because of the heat and took refuge at some house," Christine suggested.

"Aye, that could happen. Should we bake this afternoon?"

"I hate to. It's so hot. But if the men are kept searching all day, they will need to be fed this even." Christine turned from the doorway and assessed their staples. "We've plenty of ground corn but not much rye flour. The wheat flour is gone."

"Be there any meat left?" Tabitha asked.

"Nay. And we used up the fish Ben caught yesterday at luncheon."

"I've a strip of bacon in my root cellar, if that ne'er-do-well didn't get it."

Christine caught her breath and glanced at the widow, then looked pointedly toward Abby and Constance.

"Don't fuss at me," Tabitha muttered. "You should have told their father first thing this morning."

"I wanted to, but he was all in a hurry to get Ben off to the Dudleys'. He and the boys were going out the door when I arrived. And when I took his luncheon to the meetinghouse, Goodman Ackley was with him and I couldn't say anything."

Tabitha sighed and pushed herself slowly up from the chair. "Well, I'll go raid my own larder and bring over anything I think would be useful. I know there be plenty of dried beans. The Jewetts have fed me often enough this past year that I can contribute to their offering."

"Probably the other women will help as well," Christine said. "I don't like you to go over there alone."

Tabitha leaned in close. "Well now, you can't leave the children alone with that ruffian lurking about, can you?"

"Nay." Christine shuddered. She had told the outlaw she wouldn't provide for him. Leaving the Jewett girls unsupervised would be just what he needed—an opportunity for retaliation.

"Well, I know one thing, it ain't Indians has got Mahalia Ackley."

"How do you know that?"

"Ha. We've had more Indian raids than most villages, and we always know it within a short time. They're quiet until they strike, but once they begin their perfidy, there's no silencing their howling and whooping."

Christine shivered, recalling her own experience six years earlier when her home had been attacked. She well remembered the bloodthirsty screams of the savages as they wrought their destruction, killing and burning all before them. Her family had lived down the coast, near the mouth of the Piscataqua River, where her father worked a saltwater farm. The Indians had attacked and plundered several farms in the neighborhood, and Christine saw her parents and three siblings hacked down. Only after many years of prayer in the quiet convent had she found herself able to give thanks for her survival.

Sometimes she still thought it might have been better if she, too, had died that night. But nowadays, Samuel Jewett in his sermons echoed what the gentle nuns had taught her. Only last Sunday he had preached on thankfulness.

Whatever my lot, whatever my position, God has placed me here. And I thank Him.

"Take Abby with you if you are going across to your house."

Goody Deane frowned. "If you truly believe that man means to mend his ways, then you must also trust him not to carry out his threats."

"I've never said that I trust him. I only spoke to him and gave him what he asked for fear he would do violence."

The old woman nodded grudgingly. "I'd not be able to do much to protect Abby in time of need. But if I see that rascal, I'll tell her to run back here quick, and you raise the men."

"I shall."

"Abby, come with me to get a few things from my house, child. Put your shoes on."

Christine forced herself to stay away from the doorway but instead opened the barrel of parched corn and prepared to cook a mammoth kettle of samp. Goody Deane and Abby soon came back with a bit of bacon and a small sack of dried beans, which they put to soak in cold water.

"Peter Starbuck came by while we were at the cottage," Tabitha said. "I invited him to search my property if they think it needful."

Christine leaned against the frame of the loom. "I really thought they'd find her by now."

Tabitha nodded grimly. "You may as well weave. I'll watch the wee ones and the kettles."

Christine sat down and picked up her shuttle. Usually weaving brought her peace, with its monotonous movement and quiet sounds. Seeing the fabric slowly grow beneath her hands brought satisfaction. But not today. Instead she could think only of the farm wife the men searched for and the shadowy outlaw they didn't know existed.

"Lord, give me wisdom."

It flashed over her mind suddenly that in not telling Samuel about the outlaw, she had done the entire village a disservice. What if the man she had aided was responsible for Goody Ackley's disappearance?

"I must tell him." She laid her shuttle down and stood.

The doorway darkened at that moment, and Samuel Jewett entered the house. "I'm leaving John here with you, Christine. I want you all to stay inside. We fear there's foul play been done, and I don't want to risk anything happening."

John came in, stiff-legged, his lips puckered in disappointment. So his father had drawn the line. The situation had turned grim, and he had decided the boy was still a boy and shouldn't be part of this.

"Is Ben back?" she asked.

"Aye. He and the Dudley men and Charles Gardner all came into town after a runner went to ask if they'd seen Goody Ackley. I'll keep him close to me." He looked at Tabitha. "You stay, too, Goody Deane, though I know you be capable and fearless. Stay here with my family, won't you, until this is resolved." He lowered his voice. "Paine has men looking in the river now and all along the banks. The men are forming search parties. Take care, Christine. I'll see that you get word as soon as we know anything." He turned to go out.

"Samuel, wait!" Christine realized she had used his Christian name, but she hadn't time to think about that. The blood rushed to her cheeks as she stepped briskly toward him. "I must speak to you alone, sir."

His eyebrows drew together. "Is it urgent?"

"Aye. I don't think it bears on this event, but it may, and if I don't tell you and you find out later that it did, why, I shall be desolate."

He eyed her carefully then nodded. "Come outside then." He stood aside and waited for her to go out. As he followed her onto the doorstone, he closed the door behind them. "What is it? Do you know something about the goodwife's doings?"

"Nay, sir, but I know something else. Something I should have told you sooner. I would have, too, except I feared that in so doing I would endanger your children."

He turned his head slightly as though not sure he'd heard her correctly. "I don't understand."

"Forgive me. I'm rambling, but that is because I so dislike to tell you what I must. There is a man hovering about these parts. Lurking, one might say."

"A man?"

"Aye. You've heard folk say how they missed things. Foodstuffs. . .a knife. . ."

"A pair of trousers?"

She forced herself to look into his rich blue eyes. *Don't hate me, Samuel! Lord, make him understand.*

"Aye, sir. I hate to say it, but you strike true. This. . .criminal— I cannot call him less—has accosted me several times in the evening."

"How is this possible?"

"He watched the house. Both our houses. He knew our situation. The first time, I caught him peering in Tabitha's window at twilight. After that, he lingered in her garden or at the edge of the woods. He. . ." She swallowed with difficulty and looked up at Samuel.

He waited with the patience she had often seen him exercise with his children, but his eyes had a somber cast.

"He told me to bring him food. . .and other things. . .a blanket, a pair of trousers. . .and if I did not oblige him, he threatened. . ." She choked, and tears flooded her eyes.

Samuel grasped her wrist and drew her closer to him. "Christine, what are you saying? My dear girl, did he hurt you?"

She gasped and shook her head. "Nay, I promise he did not. But I was afraid, Samuel. . .Pastor." She looked away.

"Ah, Christine." He tugged gently at her arm and drew her

around the corner of the parsonage where the wall and the woodpile would hide them from view of the people on the common or coming up the street. "Tell me everything, my dear, but make haste. I must tell Constable Paine about this. The man you describe may have skulked about and harmed Goody Ackley."

"I don't think he would sir. But, then. . ."

"You said yourself you would have told me about him had you not feared him."

"Aye, it's true. He said he would hurt the children if I didn't bring him sustenance. Oh, Samuel, forgive me. I should have told you at once. I see that now, but I thought he would do it. He made these dire threats, and I took him at his word."

"Then we must assume he might harm another innocent person, namely Mahalia Ackley."

"But why?"

"Who knows? She had been to the trader. Several people saw her there this morning. Perhaps he thought to rob her of the stores she had bought, and she wouldn't give them up."

"Oh no."

"She is a stubborn woman." Samuel rested his large, strong hand on her shoulder, and the warmth of his touch comforted her. "Let us not assume the worst, but what you tell me makes me very uneasy. We will concentrate our search along the road from the trading post to the Ackley farm. Can you tell me what this man looks like? Though any stranger would be suspect under the circumstances."

"I mostly saw him in the dark, but I did get one good look at him. His beard and hair are sandy colored. He's tall. As tall as you, perhaps, and a bit thinner. His shoulders are not as broad."

Samuel gave her a bittersweet smile. "So, my gardening trousers fit him?"

"I believe they did. He might have tied them in closer than you with the bit of rope he wore for a belt."

"If he still loiters about the village, we shall find him. When did you last see him?"

"Last night. Tabitha saw him, too, though not clearly. She discovered us talking. He must have wakened her when he threw pebbles at the wall to summon me. I was telling him that he must cease and that I would not continue to do his bidding, when Tabitha came to the door and warned him off."

"She knows then."

"Aye. I told her all about it last night, and we agreed I should tell you today, but you left in such haste this morning, and then Goodman Ackley was with you at noon. . . ."

"Yes, I see. Christine, I must leave you. There is no time to be lost in searching for this woman. We shall speak more of this later."

A fresh rush of tears burst into her eyes, and she raised the hem of her apron to wipe them away. "Can you forgive me? I was foolish not to tell you right away, but I truly thought I must keep silence for the children's sake."

He touched her cheek gently, and she looked up at him. "You have nothing to fear from me. Keep close with the children, as I said, and wait for word that all is well." He hesitated a moment, then took her hand in his and pressed it. "Do not torture yourself over this. You did what seemed best."

"Father?" came a voice from the front of the parsonage.

Christine flinched, and Samuel stepped away from her.

"Father? Where are you?"

"Here, Ben." The pastor strode around the corner of the house.

Christine followed, dabbing at her damp cheeks with the apron.

"Father, come quick to the Ackleys'."

"What's happened?"

Ben stood tall as a man, but his lips trembled. "They found her. Goody Ackley is dead."

nine

"Ben, you stay here." Samuel turned around and found Christine close behind him, her eyes red rimmed from weeping. "You heard?"

"Aye. Let me go with you, if Ben will stay with Tabitha and the children. Goody Baldwin will need help to prepare the body."

Samuel nodded. "Son, do they know what happened to her?"

Ben shook his head. "I heard only that she was found and they were carrying her home in a cart. Mr. Heard told me to run and find you."

Samuel and Christine walked the mile to Roger Ackley's farm in silence. People had gathered as the word spread, and a score of men and women milled about the yard. Captain Baldwin's wife came forward to meet them.

"My husband be out back, with the constable and Brother Ackley. I be waiting for the word to tend the body, poor woman. They told me to send you around there and no other, sir."

Samuel nodded grimly. "Miss Hardin came to help, if you need assistance when the time comes."

Goody Baldwin nodded at Christine. "I can use a level-headed woman in times such as this. I expect Mrs. Dudley will be here soon, too."

Samuel left the ladies and walked around to the back of the house. James Dudley stood by his oxen, with one hand on the near ox's shoulder. Behind the team was his cart, and Baldwin, Paine, and Ackley all stared down over the sideboard, into the bed of the cart.

As Samuel approached them, Captain Baldwin looked up. "Ah, Pastor. Good. You're the man we need. Take a look, sir."

Samuel joined him beside the cart and looked down at its grisly burden. "It appears to me this work was not done by savages."

"Aye, sir," said Baldwin. "My first thought. See the wound on her temple? An Indian would have brained her with a tomahawk and scalped her."

"This looks more like a blow from a club or some such thing," Samuel agreed. "And do you see the mark around her neck?"

The men crowded in closer.

"Aye," said Paine.

"I am not a surgeon," Samuel said, "but I should think something was tight about her neck that is not there now."

"You think she were strangled?" the constable asked.

Samuel reached out and gently probed the discoloration beneath Goody Ackley's chin. "It seems likely."

Roger Ackley turned away from the sight and put his clenched fists to his eyes as though to rub away the terrible sight. "Ah, my poor, poor wife! I should have gone with her this morning."

Baldwin laid a brawny hand on his shoulder. "Easy there, Brother Roger. You cannot blame yourself."

"Can I not? She wished me to go with her to the trading post, but I told her I was too busy. If she wanted me to finish getting the hay in, she could go alone. That is what I told her. And she went."

Joseph Paine straightened, a faraway look in his eyes. "She was there when I opened this morn. She came in with a big basket, the one she often brings."

"Aye," Ackley said. "She totes things home in that, or rather, usually I do the toting."

"But where is the basket now?" Paine asked.

The men looked at each other.

"Perhaps if we find the basket, we shall know more," Baldwin suggested. "She was found in the woods, not far off the road. I shall have the men fan out from the place where she lay and see if they find her basket or any of the things she carried in it."

He left them. Samuel said to Paine, "There is nothing we can do for her but carry her inside and let the women lay her out."

"Aye. Where do you want her laid, Brother Roger?"

They mustered two more men to help them transfer the body.

Ackley ran ahead of them into the house and threw a clean sheet over the rope bed. "Place her there. I shall have to get someone to build a coffin. I would do it myself, but I am all at a loss, gentlemen." Ackley sank onto a stool, his shoulders sagging.

"I expect Charles Gardner would be willing to make the coffin," Samuel said. "Shall I speak to him for you?"

"Aye."

Christine, Goody Baldwin, Sarah Dudley and her mother-in-law, and the maid, Alice Stevens, entered the house.

"Oh, my poor, poor mistress," Alice cried when she saw the body stretched out on the bed in the corner. "I asked if she wished me to go with her this morn, but she said, 'Nay, you must finish your spinning and churn the butter.'"

Christine put an arm around her shoulders. "Mayhap you wish to go home to your mother, dear. We can tend to her."

"Nay, I must help. It is the last thing I can do for her. She were mean sometimes, but I want to do a kindness for her if I may."

"Miss Stevens," Samuel said, "pardon me for asking, but

wasn't your mistress afraid to walk a mile through forest and field alone?"

"She declared that she wasn't, sir. It be not far to the village. Oh, how I wish I had pressed her to let me go. But I was afeared she would call me lazy."

Roger Ackley rose and stumbled toward the door. "My wife was a sharp-tongued woman, but she didn't deserve this horrid end."

Baldwin cleared his throat. "Reverend, I've heard that a physician now lives at Dover Point. Shall I send a man or two to fetch him?"

"Aye, that might be good." Samuel said to Goody Baldwin, "Perhaps it is best if you ladies do not wash or dress her until we see if the physician can come. He may tell us more of her passing."

Goody Baldwin nodded. "I'll sit with her, then. If Alice wants to stay, she may. We can prepare for our duty and bake toward the morrow."

Alice sniffed. "Thank you, ma'am. I expect all the village will want to view her tomorrow. We must have gingerbread and journey cake."

Christine insisted on staying with them.

Samuel went home and ate supper, then he took his Bible to the church and studied for a scant hour.

Daniel Otis found him there at twilight. "The leech is come, sir. He's headed to the Ackleys' now."

Samuel hurried along the path beside Daniel. The physician was already in the farmhouse when he got there, and he and Daniel entered and stood in silence by Captain Baldwin and Joseph Paine to one side, while the doctor examined the body. Roger Ackley sat in a corner, declaring that he could not look on as the doctor completed his task.

The physician finished and pulled the blanket up to Goody

Ackley's neck. "I do not think she was carnally defiled."

The men let out a collective sigh.

"But she was struck in the face. See how bruised her cheek is? And strangled, that is certain. You see how her eyes have ruptured."

Samuel walked across the room and leaned over the body. He could see the fine red blood vessels in the eyes. The sight repelled him, but who knew when he would need this knowledge again?

Ackley stood and rushed outside.

"I shall go to him," said Daniel Otis.

"Reverend, you are the one they tell me tends the sick and injured?" the physician asked.

"Aye, sir. It is not my choice, nor my calling, but I do what I can in need."

"Just so. You may wish to note the white fibers in the crease of her neck."

Samuel peered where he pointed, bending closer than before. Constable Paine leaned in, too. Samuel did see a few short, fine threads clinging to the discolored skin.

The physician took a pair of tweezers from his bag and plucked one of the fibers. "That may tell you with what she was suffocated."

&.

Christine waited in the yard with the other women.

The physician was inside not ten minutes when Goodman Ackley rushed out the door and around the corner of the house.

Goodman Otis followed, more slowly. "Where is Brother Roger got to?" he asked.

Christine pointed, and Otis followed the bereaved husband.

A few minutes later, the doctor, Captain Baldwin, Paine, and Samuel emerged. Samuel headed straight toward her, and Christine felt her color rise.

"I shall go home and be with the children," he said. "Plan you to stay here all night?"

Christine looked toward Goody Baldwin, who nodded. "Aye."

"Then I shall come for you in the morning." He hesitated then said, "Walk with me a moment, Miss Hardin. I've something to say to you."

Christine walked a few steps away with him.

"My dear. . ." Samuel seemed to find inhaling difficult. "Christine, say naught to the others, but I fear the man you described to me, the outlaw who bade you feed him, is the killer."

Her lips trembled as she drew in a deep breath. "What leads you to this conclusion?"

"Nothing, except I cannot imagine any one of our own people doing this foul deed."

She also found the idea inconceivable. But still, it was hard to think that the man who had proclaimed his innocence would murder for a few groceries. Was it possible that in refusing to help him, she had condemned Mahalia Ackley to death? "Oh, Samuel, I'm afraid."

He reached toward her then let his hand fall to his side. "I'll see that the captain posts at least one man here to watch through the night. Do not try to leave here alone."

"I won't, sir."

He nodded. "I told Paine and Baldwin about the outlaw. It is time to gather the men of the village, warn them, and plan how we shall find this felon."

"You will be sure he is not harmed, won't you?"

Samuel looked at her strangely, his forehead wrinkled between his brows. "Christine, you cannot believe him innocent of this."

"But I can. He at least should have a fair trial. No one has proven him guilty of anything. I myself would testify that he has pilfered and manipulated and intimidated, and, yes, stolen. But I do not say he has killed. Not until I see proof."

"You seem certain. If you fear him, as you told me you do, how can you think him incapable of this act?"

"I cannot fully answer that." She tried to picture the man's haunting face once more, and a shudder ran through her. "I'm not fully persuaded that he is innocent, but neither am I positive of his guilt."

Samuel closed his eyes for a moment. When he opened them, he nodded. "As you wish. I shall speak for him because you ask me to. It is right for him to be fairly tried, as you say. 'Vengeance is mine,' saith the Lord. I shall admonish the men not to mistreat him if they catch him. But I tell you, it stirs my wrath when I think of what he said to you—when I remember he swore to mutilate my dear little children." His voice cracked, and he looked away.

Christine's heart wrenched. "Oh, Samuel." She longed to touch him, but several people still milled about the yard, and there was no surer way to ruin a minister's reputation than to let him be seen touching—or being touched by—a woman not his wife. "My dear Samuel," she whispered, "thank you. I shall pray that God will bring this all to rights."

"Your faith is stronger than mine at this moment, though I know you speak truth." He turned and took the road to the village.

Christine watched him go, her heart aching.

❧

The Dudley men stopped by the farmhouse in the morning just after sunup on their way to the village. Christine and Goody Baldwin went with them, leaving Alice Stevens and Goody Dudley with Roger Ackley and the corpse.

As Christine had feared, the constable raised a posse to

beat the forest all about. Christine watched them come and go on the common. The Jewett children fretted to go outside and play, but she would not let them.

Goody Deane was nearly as bad. She sat in the chair, darning stockings and muttering all morning. At last she called to Christine, "Do something, lass! Weave or bake or scrub, but don't stand there in the light of the doorway."

Christine turned and saw all four children—Ben had gone with the men—staring at her. Tempting as the loom was, she knew she hadn't the right to please herself that day. If she retreated in solitary brooding and weaved the hours away, the children would suffer.

She forced a smile. "Come, children. Alice Stevens bade me bring a cheese and some dried apples back with me. Let us see what we can make special for dinner. Won't your father and Ben be surprised if we have dried apple tart waiting for them?"

Too late she remembered they had no wheat flour, so they crumbled maple sugar and oats over the apples instead of a crust. "A sprinkle of cinnamon and bit of lard." She let Constance cover the Dutch oven. "There now. Stand back, and I shall cover it in coals." Once it was baking, she was hard pressed to come up with another project.

Goody Deane finished her darning and coaxed Abby and Constance to sit with her and try to knit. "You shall make your dollies a fine new coverlet," she promised them.

John got down his wooden soldiers and animals. He even let Ruth play with a few, and so the hours passed.

All the while, Christine's thoughts roiled round and round. Was the outlaw guilty of murder? How would they ever know for certain, unless he confessed? Had her hesitation to expose him brought about Mahalia Ackley's death? She sent many prayers heavenward, until they all seemed to run together.

Father, keep Samuel and Ben safe. Let justice be done. Forgive me if I did wrong.

But she knew not whether to pray they found the outlaw or not.

ଛ

Samuel and Ben tramped through the woods between the gristmill and the brickworks. They penetrated every thicket and peered up into every tree. They could hear other men not far away doing the same.

Paine and Baldwin had done a good job of organizing the search, Samuel thought. As well as any man could do. Every structure in the village had been searched, from the meetinghouse on down to the lowest root cellar. No trace of the man had been found. One man had gone so far as to suggest Miss Hardin's outlaw was a phantom, made up to let them give up looking for the murderer among themselves.

Samuel had silenced that talk quickly, saying Miss Hardin was as honest and as staunch as they come. Baldwin, Paine, and the Dudley men backed him up, and the search resumed.

As he hunted the elusive man, Samuel wondered if Christine had told him all. She had met the outlaw at least half a dozen times, he judged. Did she sympathize with him? Had she gone so far as to set her affections on him? It was unthinkable, and yet the inkling was there. Samuel raised his corn knife and slashed viciously at a thicket of brambles.

Lord, calm my spirit.

With a sudden start, he realized that a man crouched in the bushes, his hands raised before his face.

Samuel froze with his arm over his head, ready to strike the brambles again.

The man roared and leaped at him.

ten

"Wait!" Samuel cried.

His adversary plunged forward.

Samuel swung the corn knife downward at the man's arm. His breath whooshed out of him as his adversary's body hit him, knocking him to the ground. Samuel lost his grip on the corn knife and grappled with the man, rolling over in the thicket.

He heard yelling, but he didn't dare pause to make sense of it. As he continued to struggle, the man's grip seemed to weaken. After a moment, Samuel felt strong hands tugging at his arms, lifting him off his opponent.

Stephen Dudley and Charles Gardner jumped on the stranger, hauling him to his feet.

Samuel realized that Richard Dudley had pulled him away from the man and was supporting him as they watched. "Are you well, Parson?"

"Aye, Richard. Thank you. He had a knife in his hand."

"Looks like you got the better of him." Richard stooped and picked up Samuel's long corn knife.

"I regret that," Samuel said. "I had only a moment to act, and I struck hard, I fear."

The captured man bled profusely from a deep gash on his forearm, where Samuel had slashed through his sleeve.

He fumbled with the knot that tied his handkerchief about his neck. "Here, Charles. Hold him steady, and I'll wrap his wound."

The man snarled as he approached.

"Easy, now," Charles said, yanking him up straighter. "The parson is a healer. Let him see to your arm."

"He like to ha' cut my arm off!"

Stephen picked up a bone-handled knife. "And you never planned to hurt him with this, I suppose."

Richard put his own kerchief in Samuel's hand, and the pastor moved in warily and pulled the man's sleeve up. The cut went clear to the bone.

"You'd best let him sit," he told Charles. "I'll wrap it tight and try to stop the bleeding, but he needs to be sewn up."

"Should we fetch that doctor back from the Point?" Stephen asked.

Samuel swallowed hard. He was a little light-headed. "Perhaps so. I could do it, but I fear my hands are not steady now, and I wouldn't do so neat a job, I'm sure."

"Reverend?" Captain Baldwin shouted from fifty yards away through the trees. "You faring well over there?"

"Come on over here, Captain," Richard bellowed. "We've got a prisoner for you."

Samuel felt a timid touch at his elbow. He turned and found Ben staring at him with glassy eyes. "Father! Are you hurt?"

"Nay, son." Samuel realized he was shaking all over. He pulled Ben toward him and gave him a swift hug. "I'm fine."

"I didn't see him," Ben choked.

"Neither did I until it was too late."

The captain arrived with half a dozen other men from the search. "Well, now, what have we here?" Baldwin asked with a pleased air. "Caught a skulker, have you, Preacher?"

"He was hiding in the thicket," Samuel said.

"Aye, he went at the pastor with this." Stephen held up the stranger's knife.

"Hey!" Daniel Otis stepped forward. "That's my knife

that I lost a couple of weeks ago. . .or rather my knife that someone stole."

Richard clapped Samuel on the shoulder. "You'd best get home and rest, Pastor. We'll lock up this worthless excuse for a man."

"Aye," said Baldwin. "Let's march him over to Heard's garrison. We can lock him in the smokehouse there until a magistrate tells us what to do with him."

"I didn't do anything," the man cried. "This barbarous preacher tried to cut my head off, and I didn't do anything!"

"Nothing?" Baldwin grasped the front of the man's shirt and pulled him up close, nose to nose with him. "What about the goodwife who was throttled yesterday, hey?"

The man's lips trembled. "I know nothing of that. I swear."

"Be careful what you swear to," said Charles. "Now, come along."

❧

The door latch rattled. Christine jumped up from the bench by the loom, her heart racing. She had laid the bar in place before sitting down with Abby to give her a lesson at weaving. It seemed odd to bar the door in the daytime, but with the men out looking for the killer, she would not have been surprised if the outlaw tried to take shelter there.

Tabitha and the children all stared toward the door. A loud knocking resounded through the house.

"Who is it?" she cried.

"It's I, Christine. Let me in."

She sprang forward at Samuel's voice and grabbed the bar. The door flew open. She felt tears spring to her eyes as Samuel and Ben entered.

"We found your thief." Samuel headed for the water bucket and helped himself to a dipperful.

Christine put one hand to her lips. "Is he. . ."

"He's alive."

"Father sliced him with his corn knife," Ben blurted.

The girls gasped.

John jumped up and ran to his brother. "Really? Did you see it? Tell us what happened."

"There, now. Hush, John." Samuel sank down on the bench at the table.

Christine noticed blood on his hands and sleeve. "Sir, are you wounded?"

"Nay. The blood is not mine." He ran his hand over his eyes. "If I weren't so tired, I would get up and wash."

She stepped toward him and stopped, wanting to ask all sorts of questions. She crumpled her apron between her hands. "May I bring you something, sir?"

"Aye. There's no chocolate, I suppose."

"Nay, sir, but I can fix you some strong mint tea."

"I suppose that will do."

While the tea steeped, she brought a basin of warm water and a facecloth. Samuel looked up at her and murmured his thanks then began to rinse the blood from his hands. She set a plate of samp with a slice of cheese and a portion of boiled cabbage before him and fixed one for Ben as well. The boy sat down and began to eat ravenously.

Samuel looked up at her, his eyelids drooping. "Thank you. I'm about played out, I fear, with all that's happened these last two days. And tomorrow we shall bury Goody Ackley." He sighed and reached for his spoon.

She bit her lip and forced herself to keep silence.

"Did Father really catch the murderer?" John sidled onto the bench next to Ben.

"Keep your peace, John," Samuel said. "We caught a man lurking in the woods, but we know not whether he killed Goody Ackley. That shall be determined when the magistrate comes."

Christine cleared her throat. "When will that be?"

"I don't know. Captain Baldwin took charge of the prisoner. They're taking him to the Heards' to lock him up. I expect to hear more tomorrow."

Goody Deane pushed her knitting into her workbag and rose. "And tonight you should rest, sir. Now that the blackguard is in custody, I shall go home."

"Nay, you and Christine must have your supper first. You've stayed here all day, and I doubt you had much rest with these four children cooped up here with you."

Christine could see that Tabitha moved slowly, as though her stiff joints ached. "Sit down now with the men, dear lady. Have some food, and as soon as I've fed the children I shall take you home. Abby and John can do the washing up tonight, if I pour the hot water for them. Can you not, children?"

John nodded somberly, and Abby hurried to her side. "We can do it, Miss Christine. Will you let me weave some more tomorrow?"

Christine smoothed Abby's hair and smiled. She was glad the girl was more excited about weaving than about the man whom Samuel had apparently injured. "Of course I will. If you like it, you'll soon be making material for your own petticoats and skirts."

❧

The next morning, Samuel ate his breakfast and prepared to go over to the meetinghouse for an hour or two's study before Mahalia Ackley's funeral service. He paused in the doorway with his Bible in his hand and watched Christine place several biscuits and a dish of gruel in a basket. "May I inquire your purpose this morning?" he asked.

She looked up and paused. "I thought to take something to the prisoner."

Samuel stepped away from the door and stood for a moment,

regarding her in confusion.

"Mrs. Heard will prepare something for him to eat, I'm sure. The captain will have set a watch over him. You needn't trouble yourself on his behalf."

Christine stood still, her eyes downcast. "Forgive me. I should have asked your permission first. I only want to be sure he is being treated well. It was cooler last night than it has been in many weeks, and I thought he might need a blanket tonight. And I wondered if they let him wash, or whether anyone will tend his wound, which you—" She stopped abruptly and turned away, her hand at her lips.

"Which I caused." Samuel stepped toward her, acutely aware of his children watching. "Christine, do you think we would let him languish unfed, untreated? I shall go myself to dress his wound after the service if need be, but it was Baldwin's intention yesterday to fetch the physician back again to tend him and stitch up his arm."

Her shoulders jerked.

Samuel stepped closer and lowered his voice. "Christine! Think you that I injured him on purpose? He tried to kill me, lass. I struck in self-defense. I regret it turned out this way, but that is what happened. Do you care about this felon so much? Please, do not imagine that I gladly maimed him."

"You are angry with me." She turned, and he saw a tear clinging to her lashes.

"Nay. But I shall be if you go to the Heards'. Would you leave the children alone to go and comfort the prisoner the morning we bury his victim?"

She caught her breath. "How can you say that? You forbade John to call him a murderer until such is proven, yet you say it yourself."

He stared at her. Something twisted in his heart. Could she possibly have formed an ill-advised attachment to the man who bullied her and perhaps strangled her neighbor? "I forbid you to go to him."

She straightened her shoulders, and her eyes flashed. For an instant he feared she would challenge his right to speak so and go anyway.

Dear God, how have we come to this? Meek Christine defying me! Please, let us not show ill will before the children.

He swallowed hard and tried to frame a gentle overture, but Christine opened her mouth first. "Very well, sir." Her posture drooped. She took the food out of the basket and folded the napkin.

He stood unmoving for a moment. The children still watched. The quiet in the room bespoke their attention, and he could feel their stares. He cleared his throat. "Thank you for that. I shall go at once to the garrison and inquire whether the prisoner needs food or medical care."

Leaving his Bible on the table, he set out with long, purposeful strides.

❧

Christine sent all of the children but Ruth to the river to fill the water buckets. Mr. Dudley did not need Ben's labor this morning, since all of the villagers would attend the funeral service. Ben would watch John and the girls, and the brief excursion would do them all good.

As soon as they were out the door, she crumpled into the chair by the hearth and pulled her apron up to cover her face. Her sobs came unbidden, shocking her. She must stop weeping before the children returned.

After a few minutes, she felt a small, warm hand on her wrist.

"Why you cryin', Miss 'Stine?"

She raised her chin and wiped her eyes. Ruth stared up at her with wide blue eyes, as troubled as her father's.

Christine clasped the little girl to her. "I'm sorry, dear. Your papa is right. There is no need to worry."

Did she weep for the outlaw or for herself? She could not tell. Perhaps it was for the straining of the fragile tie between her and Samuel.

Things had changed between them. Two days ago, when she told him about the outlaw, he had responded considerately, almost tenderly. But now his tone had hardened. He thought her foolish to have acted as she did, aiding the thief and concealing his existence. Once, she had felt Samuel respected her and counted her a friend. Had that changed? Would she ever enjoy his high regard again?

She managed to smile at Ruth. "Come, let us set the bread to rise while we are at the service."

❧

Samuel returned to the parsonage just long enough to retrieve his Bible before the funeral procession reached the common. Christine had all the children scrubbed and turned out in their Sunday best, and Goody Deane had come to walk over to the meetinghouse with them.

"You needn't worry about McDowell," Samuel said.

"Who?" Christine stared at him.

"The prisoner. The Heards will feed him. He is well taken care of, and the physician dressed his wound this morning."

"Ah." She ducked her head and untied her apron.

So. . .she hadn't known even his name. Somehow that lightened Samuel's spirit.

He went out and hurried to the meetinghouse steps. James Dudley's cart carried the coffin, and all of the neighbors who lived in that direction followed slowly behind. Elder William Heard cut across the green past the stocks. Samuel greeted him. Heard went inside and brought out the large conch shell they used to call the people to meeting and began to blow.

Other people came from up and down the village street, walking with somber, measured steps. Samuel waited until all the people had gathered on the green before the meetinghouse. The pallbearers lifted the casket out of the cart. Roger Ackley, his face set like stone, joined him on the steps, and Samuel led them into the building.

After the service and the burial, the villagers melted away to their farms and businesses, with no prolonged socializing. Many had already lost two days' work due to Goody Ackley's death and could not afford to give up more.

Ben went home with the Dudleys, and Samuel walked home with the children and Christine for his dinner. While she put the food on, he walked about the garden, observing the abundant crops brought on by hot, steamy days and occasional gentle rains.

When Constance came out to call him to the dinner table, he took her hand and walked in with her.

"We have corn to pick," he told Christine, "and a few cucumbers."

"The children and I can do it this afternoon."

"I'll stay a short while and help." He made the decision as he spoke. Working together in the garden might give him a chance to speak to Christine again out of earshot of his offspring.

To his surprise, he had no need to make an opportunity. After dinner, she put baskets in the children's hands and sent them into the garden, then she turned to him as she tied the strings of her bonnet. "I fear this business has caused a rift between us, sir, and I do not like it. Can you forgive me?"

He stepped closer and looked into her serious hazel eyes. "As I told you two days past, there is nothing to forgive. You acted as you thought best. Indeed, you may have saved the family from tragedy."

A flush stained her cheeks, but she did not look away from him. "I meant, forgive me for my ill-considered actions. . .and my words. . .this morning. I was wrong to put this man—McDowell, you call him—ahead of you and the children."

"Nay, not so remiss. It is only Christian charity to see that the lowest—widows, orphans, prisoners—are cared for."

"But—" She bit her lip.

"What is it, Christine?"

"I did feel animosity this morning when you spoke to me. Perhaps it lies beyond my right to mention it."

Samuel sighed. "Nay, I hope you will come to me with anything that concerns you. And you are not far off the mark." He looked out over the field, where the children raced to fill their baskets. "I fear I misconstrued your actions today. It is I who needs pardon."

"Pastor, you cannot think I imagined. . .that I cared for him in any but the most humane way."

He smiled as the bittersweet reality struck him again. She was right. A new formality that had not been there before separated them. "You called me by my Christian name not so long ago."

Her color deepened. "Forgive me. I spoke in haste and agitation."

"I do not wish to forgive that slip, Christine. It was pleasant to hear. . .and to think we were friends."

She couldn't look at him then, or so it seemed. Had he spoken too plainly? For he could no longer deny that Christine, who had come to them a shy, tall, awkward girl with the plainest of features two years ago and more, had become a responsible, caring woman who had found a place in his heart.

"If you count me as a friend," she said softly, watching the children, "then please take my word. I sympathized with him, it is true. At times he almost convinced me he was innocent.

But even if he were the vilest of men, he ought not to be locked up and left unattended while he bled and suffered. My faith in our people was small that day. I had seen them go out vowing to find the murderer and flay him alive."

"That is true. I spoke to several of the men, in an attempt to calm them. I'm glad it was I who stumbled upon the fugitive. I should hate to think what some of the men would have done if they had found him first."

"But we still don't know if he had anything to do with Mahalia Ackley's death. Yet today at the graveside, I heard murmuring that the prisoner should be taken out and hung at once."

Samuel drew in a deep, uneasy breath. "You are right. There is unrest in the village. Captain Baldwin has posted a double guard at the Heards' smokehouse to be sure the man is not molested. And I. . ." He watched her closely. "I have agreed to go to Portsmouth as one of the delegation that seeks to bring a magistrate here to try McDowell."

She was silent for a moment; then she looked up at him. "You agree with me then? That the truth must be uncovered?"

"Of course. I would want nothing less. But McDowell refuses to admit to anything, even stealing Daniel Otis's knife, which we found in his possession. Are you willing to accept the truth if it be not to your liking?"

She nodded. "The thing that would upset me would be injustice—condemning a man before his case is proven."

"Then I promise you I shall do all in my power to see that the truth is found and upheld. And will you make a promise to me?"

Her brow furrowed. "What is it?"

"That you will never lie to me or hold back information that will affect this family again."

Tears sprang into her eyes. "Oh, yes."

He reached out and wiped away the single tear that rolled down her cheek. "I know you went to great lengths not to tell an outright lie, my dear. I see that now."

"Yes, but you are right. I did deceive you about it. The trousers..."

He chuckled. "Aye. McDowell was wearing them when he jumped on me. I never noticed until Paine and Baldwin marched him away."

"I've made you a new pair, from some cloth that Jane Gardner gave me. It's coarse material, but they will make good workaday trousers."

He felt his smile growing, and he didn't try to hold it back. "Do you assure me that you could never have tender feelings for a man like that?"

"I do, sir."

He arched his eyebrows. "Do you recall that you have many times told me you couldn't feel that way for any man and that you wished to remain unmarried?"

A cloud descended on her brow. "Aye, sir."

They stood looking at each other for a long moment. Her trust and championing of the outlaw might be misplaced empathy but surely not affection, Samuel mused. Still, he mustn't assume that she had developed deep personal feelings for himself. He was her employer—of sorts—and the father of the children she cared for. He had exercised the utmost discretion to show her nothing beyond Christian love.

But someday, he would ask her if she still held to her declared purpose of remaining single. Because he was beginning to hope she would not.

"Father! I've filled my basket. Look!" Abby ran toward them.

Ruth ran along behind her, holding up her smaller basket. "Me, too! Look, Miss 'Stine."

Christine knelt and gathered Ruth into the curve of her arm. "Well done, girls."

Samuel smiled. "Here we've stood idle while you children worked. I shall stay and help Miss Christine husk the corn."

"You shall do no such thing." She stood and brushed off her skirt. "You shall go and study, and we shall husk the corn."

eleven

The next day, the minister and Ben left with William Heard
and Joseph Paine for Portsmouth, pledging to bring back
a magistrate or the promise of one's soon arrival. Christine
took her quilt and her few extra garments and moved into
the parsonage, expecting the pastor to return by Saturday
evening.

The pilfering in the village had ceased, but gossip ran
rampant. Tabitha and Jane brought Christine reports of
what was whispered at clotheslines behind the cottages.
The outlaw the Reverend Jewett had captured was behind
it all. Goodwives cudgeled their memories and pulled out
anecdotes describing items they had lost over the past few
months and ascribed them to McDowell's evil doings.
Christine had to laugh when she heard old Mrs. Squires say
McDowell had surely stolen her hoarded pouch of coins. The
woman's savings had disappeared more than a year earlier,
long before McDowell came to Cochecho, and on the same
day, as it happened, that her knave of a son had run off.

Christine, ten-year-old John, and the three Jewett girls
spent a quiet day on Friday, working in the garden and about
the house. Abby had a weaving lesson in the afternoon, and
Goody Deane came over to partake of supper with them.
Christine urged the old woman to spend the night with
them, but she refused, saying she would sleep better in her
own bed.

In truth, Christine was anxious about where she would sleep
that night. No matter what the reverend had said before he

left, she could not stay in his room. The very thought made perspiration break out on her brow. His chamber and that occupied by his daughters were built the year before, added on to the parsonage by the men of the parish. The cramped family had sorely needed the extra space. However, Christine was sure the parson must feel quite lonely now, with a fine bedchamber all to himself. She thought it a pity that he and his dear wife had slept on a pallet in the great room, and the new chambers were only constructed after Elizabeth's death.

John solved her problem when bedtime neared. His tone held a note of jest, but Christine felt he half meant it when he said, "I shall miss old Ben tonight. What shall I do, tossing about all alone up there in the loft?"

"What, afraid of the dark?" Abby asked.

"Nay."

Christine said, "I expect he feels as you would if Constance and Ruth were elsewhere tonight." She smiled at John. "I tell you what. Would you like to sleep down here by the hearth, as you and Ben used to do when you were younger? We shan't keep a fire tonight—'tis too warm. You may set up your wooden soldiers on the stones, and I shall climb the ladder and sleep above."

"You, Miss Christine?" Constance asked, her eyes round with wonder.

"Aye. Not much more than a year past I slept up there every night with you and your sisters. Have you forgotten?"

Constance's face darkened. "Aye. When Mama was with us."

"That's right." Christine infused her voice with cheerfulness. "And I shall do it again tonight."

"May we sleep up there with you?" Abby asked eagerly.

"Me, too," Ruth cried.

Christine caught her breath. Would the pastor approve? She had feared that the funeral they attended the previous day had reminded the children strongly of their mother's service last year. The diversion of sleeping in the loft would certainly keep the little girls from thinking about the morbid events they had witnessed lately.

"All right. And when we've settled our bedding up there, I shall tell you all a story, and then John shall come down and blow out the candles, and we shall all sleep well."

It happened just that way, and even Christine did not lie awake long. After a sincere prayer for the safety of the men who went to Portsmouth and a petition for the outlaw's soul, she drifted into slumber.

She had barely dressed and got the fire going the next morning, when a quiet knock came at the door.

John scurried to open it and admitted Stephen Dudley, who was now seventeen years old and living quietly with his parents and sister. However, from his tenth year to his fifteenth, he had dwelt among the Algonquin in Quebec and had made the choice to return on his own a few months after Christine had come to Cochecho. "Good day, Miss Hardin."

"Good morning, Stephen. You're about early." Christine noticed that he carried a large basket. "May I help you?"

"Be the pastor at home?"

"Nay. He's gone to Portsmouth with Mr. Heard and Mr. Paine and Ben to fetch the magistrate."

Stephen's mouth tightened. "I'd best go to Captain Baldwin then, I suppose."

Christine's curiosity was piqued. "Is there anything I can do? The pastor will return this evening, I expect."

"Some of us poked about yesterday afternoon, near the place where Pastor Jewett flushed out the knave, and we found a camp."

"A camp?"

"Aye. Someone had stayed there. Built a fire and made a

bed of pine boughs." He pulled a dirty, ragged blanket out of the basket. "This were nearby."

Christine drew in her breath. Filthy though it was, she recognized the old blanket she had left for the outlaw.

"And this." Stephen lifted the basket toward her. "I found the basket beside his fire ring. Think you it belonged to Goody Ackley?"

Christine grasped the corner of the table to steady herself. The basket indeed resembled the one she had often seen the late Mahalia Ackley carry about the village.

"It may well be hers. Perhaps you should take it to her husband and ask him."

Stephen hesitated. "I could do that."

Christine sensed that, in spite of his adventures and his solitary travel for hundreds of miles through the woods, the young man was reluctant to face Roger Ackley alone. He had probably hoped the minister would accompany him.

"I could go with you," she offered.

Stephen's expression cleared at once, telling her she had assumed correctly. Stephen disliked the thought of confronting the bereaved man and perhaps suffering further disparagement from his acerbic tongue.

"John," Christina said to the boy, who had hovered near and listened to their exchange, "run yonder and fetch Goody Deane, if you please. Your sisters will be rising soon, and I don't like to leave you four alone while I run this errand."

While John ran across the street, she hung up her apron and fetched her shawl. Though the sun was well up, the air promised to be less stifling than it had been lately. She wished she had some fresh baking to take to the widower, but she had none.

"Shall I ask Captain Baldwin to accompany us?" Stephen asked.

It would take him time to go to Baldwin's house and back, but it sounded like a wise idea to Christine. "Perhaps you could go now and speak to him. I shall stay until Goody Deane is here, and then I'll meet you on the path to Goodman Ackley's. Oh, and Stephen. . ."

He had turned to leave, but swung around to look at her.

"You needn't take the blanket. That came from this house."

"Ah." He held it out.

She took it with distaste and wadded it into the corner where dirty laundry awaited her ministrations.

Stephen left, carrying the basket, and Christine set about cooking cornmeal mush for the children's breakfast. John soon came racing back, with Tabitha Deane hobbling along behind him.

Christine stood in Goodman Ackley's house a half hour later with the owner, Stephen, Captain Baldwin, and Alice Stevens. Christine was surprised that they found Alice there, with the mistress of the house dead and buried, but on their arrival Alice left her work in the garden and joined them inside.

Baldwin handed the basket Stephen had found to Goodman Ackley. "Be this not the market basket your wife always carried to the trader?"

Alice gasped and covered her hand with her mouth, staring at the basket.

Ackley appeared to study it with care, fingering the woven reeds. "It might be that," he said at last.

Baldwin fixed his gaze on the maid. "What say you, Miss Stevens? Be this your late mistress's basket?"

"Aye. The mistress had it on her arm the day she left here." Alice looked away.

"Young Dudley found it in a thicket near where we caught the prisoner," Baldwin said. "There were a blanket and the remains of a fire near it."

Goodman Ackley's eyes took on an interest. "Then he did it. That man, McDowell. It were his camp, where he lurked. And he went about his nefarious business from there, no doubt."

"But your wife's body was found at least a mile from there, much nearer this house."

"He stole her basket of provisions," Ackley said, nodding eagerly. He looked again at the basket, peering inside it. "Yes, it's Mahalia's. Don't you see? She'd been to the trading post, and he attacked her as she made her way home. He took what she'd bought. Ye didn't find any packages of food lying about, did you?"

Baldwin looked at Stephen, and he shook his head. "I'll go with Stephen and examine the spot myself," the captain said. "But whatever foodstuff the thief didn't use may have been ravaged by animals."

Stephen said nothing.

Christine hoped this evidence would not hang McDowell. It seemed rather thin to her, when a man's life was at stake. As they were leaving, she said to Baldwin, "Mayhap we should keep the basket as evidence for the magistrate?"

"Aye, you may be right. Do you mind, Ackley?"

The farmer shook his head.

They set out along the road to the village. When they were out of sight of the Ackley farm, Stephen said to the captain, "What think ye, sir?"

Baldwin frowned. "I'm not sure yet, Stephen. Let us wait and see what the future brings."

Christine looked at them in confusion. "I don't understand."

The captain stopped and eyed her soberly. "Stephen told me that he and his brother went over that area in the woods yesterday, after the funeral service. They found the outlaw's camp then."

"But. . .Stephen only came to us this morning with the basket."

"Aye. The basket were not there when they went yesterday."

"I only went back this morning at dawn to be sure we hadn't overlooked anything," Stephen said. "We'd found the blanket, but it was an old rag." He hesitated, throwing her a look of embarrassment.

"Aye, so it was," she said. "That is why I gave him that one when he demanded a blanket, and not one of the parson's or Goody Deane's good quilts."

Baldwin nodded. "When Stephen came to me this morning with that basket, I knew something was up."

"It was lying right beside the blanket," Stephen said. "We'd have tripped over it if it had been there yesterday."

Baldwin fixed them both with a somber look. "Let us keep this among the three of us. We shall let the parson and the constable be privy to it when they return, but none other, saving the magistrate. Agreed?"

Stephen and Christine nodded gravely.

❧

Samuel strode swiftly with his son along the dusty road toward Cochecho. Paine and Heard had elected to stay in Portsmouth over the weekend in order to do some business on Monday, but Samuel had to be back in time to preach his sermons on Sunday. He and Ben had taken a boat to Dover Point but had to walk the last few miles to the village. They should reach home before sunset.

Home. Thoughts of the humble parsonage now included Christine, and the knowledge that she and the other children waited there for his return. He knew she took good care of John and the three girls in his absence, just as he knew she prayed for his safety. She had perhaps done a washing today, or maybe she had baked. She had surely prepared the meals and supervised the children in sweeping the floor and washing the dishes. If nothing pressing called her attention, she might be sitting right now mending, or more likely, weaving.

Christine. The parsonage would not be home without her.

And yet, he might lose her soon. Samuel felt keenly the possibility that she might leave his employ. She had said nothing to that effect, and yet. . . He had promised to help find the truth in McDowell's case. If the outlaw were proved innocent, would Christine champion him and perhaps set her affections on him? It was unthinkable. . . . The man was a thief, if nothing more. And yet Samuel still considered it.

On the other hand, if McDowell were found guilty of Mahalia Ackley's murder, Christine might be angry. In spite of her meekness yesterday morning, did she resent Samuel's role in capturing the outlaw? Would she deny his guilt even if the magistrate and a jury declared it? If so, she might not wish to be around the pastor anymore.

The thought caused him to slow his steps. Christine now held a firm place in his heart, as well as in his home. He didn't want that to change, unless. . . How good it would be for the children if she were his wife!

"Father?" Ben was eyeing him carefully.

"What is it, son?"

"You seem distracted, Father."

"Aye. Long thoughts. Let us hasten. I long to be home with my family."

Ben seemed to have no objection, and they hurried forward.

An hour later, they reached the village. Samuel's steps were slower. It had been a long and tiring day. But his spirits rose when he saw Constance and John come running around the corner of his house. Beyond, Christine followed more slowly from the vegetable patch with Ruth clinging to her hand.

Samuel swung Constance up into his arms with a grunt. "You'll soon be too large for me to pick up, young lady." He kissed her and set her on the ground. "Did you children behave?"

"Yes, Father," said Constance.

"Of course!" John fell into step with Ben. "What did you see in Portsmouth?"

As Christine and Ruth approached them, Samuel slowed and let the children go into the house. "Good evening." He stooped and hauled Ruth into his arms. "Where's Abby?" He straightened holding the child.

Christine smiled. "She's at the loom. I fear I've taught her almost too well. She has a good touch for it, and I can barely coax her from her weaving at mealtime."

"That will pass when she's woven a few yards of cloth," Samuel said. "All is at peace here?"

"Aye. I've somewhat to tell you, though."

They reached the doorstone, and Samuel set Ruth inside the doorway. "There, now, tell Abby that Father would like some tea." He turned back to evaluate Christine's sober expression. Her hazel eyes held suppressed excitement tinged with anxiety. "What is it?"

"Stephen Dudley found Goody Ackley's market basket near the outlaw's camp in the woods. But he and Richard had been there yesterday, and he's certain the basket was not there then."

Samuel inhaled deeply and looked out over the village. The outlaw again. Christine must care more for McDowell than she had admitted, if she could think and speak of nothing else. He had been gone a day and a half, yet the first topic she broached when he returned home was that worthless thief.

He sighed. "Well, the magistrate will come as soon as he can."

"When?"

"Probably not next week. He's holding court in Portsmouth and has several cases scheduled. He told William Heard to hold the prisoner until he comes. A lawyer will come, too, to represent the accused."

He wished this business was over with and McDowell gone.

"That is well," she said. "Are you hungry?"

"Aye, but the supper hour is past, and I must get to my studies."

"You shall eat something first. I saved portions for you and Ben." She went inside.

Lord, truly, she seems just what I need. Give me patience.

Samuel followed her and let the comfort of home refresh his tired soul.

twelve

On Sunday morning, since Brother Heard had not returned from Portsmouth, Samuel allowed Ben to blow the shell and call the people to worship. They came from the farms, from the fishermen's cottages, and the garrison houses. Samuel preached with passion, although his hours for preparing the sermon had been severely curtailed that week. His words on justice thundered through the rafters.

Christine sat very straight and still in the new boxed-in pew, center and front, just below the pulpit. Her eyes were fixed on him so intently that Samuel had to force himself not to look down there too often. When he did, though, he saw that John was wriggling, and Christine paid the boy no mind. Half of Samuel's mind hoped Brother Wentworth would see and rap John smartly on the head with his staff. The other half hoped he wouldn't, and thus save him the embarrassment of having the entire congregation know that his son had misbehaved in church.

At the noontime break, he shook hands with each of the church members and greeted them. Several of the men asked about his journey to Portsmouth and when the magistrate would arrive.

At last he left the church doorway and found Christine on the green with the children about her. "Why don't you invite your friends to eat their dinner at the parsonage today?" he asked.

"Oh, Father!" Abby cried with shining eyes. "We'll get to play with the babies again."

"Hush now." He looked only at Christine. Her hazel eyes met his gaze with confusion.

"But this is a quiet hour for you, sir, when you can eat your dinner in peace and meditate on your message for this afternoon."

"I thought you might like to ask the Gardners and the Dudleys over. You've not had a chance to visit with them lately."

"Only if you wish it, sir. I can wait."

"I wish it."

She did not bounce about laughing, like Abby and Constance, or giggle in glee, like Ruth, but he thought her quiet smile showed a pleasure he seldom saw on her face. Why did he not more often seek to please her?

"Thank you. I shall invite them."

Fifteen minutes later, he found himself at his table surrounded by Richard Dudley, Charles Gardner, and their wives. The mothers held their babies on their laps while they ate the food they'd brought in their baskets, and his own children waited for the plates to be washed. When Christine began to serve them, Samuel said swiftly, "Sit down, Christine, and enjoy the company. Let Abby and Constance do that."

The unaccustomed fellowship brought a glow of pleasure to her face. He had not always been so stern that his family thought it ungodly to enjoy the company of other believers on Sunday, Samuel reflected. When Elizabeth lived, they used to have large groups of people into their home for Sabbath-day lunches, especially in the cold winter. But lately he had pleaded the need to rest or study.

Seeing the three young women together again brought back memories of the days they had all lived in his home. And now two of the young captives were settled, with good, God-fearing husbands. He smiled as he thought how Elizabeth had despaired of ever finding a husband for Christine. She had been so withdrawn, so aloof, to the point of being prickly. And women like Goody Ackley had whispered that no man would ever offer for the tall, homely girl.

Odd how one's perspective changed. He no longer noticed how tall Christine was, except perhaps when she stood beside one of the young children. When he spoke to her and their eyes were not more than a few inches off being level, it didn't bother him. And would anyone call her homely now? She seemed to have softened somehow.

Perhaps it was the more becoming hairstyle she had adopted under Jane Gardner's urging, or the gentle manner she exhibited with his children. She seldom scowled, and when she smiled, her features smoothed into lines, if not pretty, then at least agreeable. He only knew that lately he'd begun to think she had improved her appearance. Her deportment was almost regal. Her features. . .why, a man could look at that honest, straight nose and those thoughtful eyes every day and not tire of it. In fact, he did!

Richard Dudley nudged him with his elbow. "That right, Pastor?"

"What?"

Richard chuckled.

"I'm sorry," Samuel said. "I was lost in thought, I fear." He hoped they did not see the flush he felt reddening his face beneath his beard. A sidelong glance at Charles Gardner told him otherwise. He'd been caught, no question. Caught staring at Christine.

She jumped up suddenly. "Let me get the teakettle."

Samuel thought her ears had gone quite pink. Yes, she had a most interesting face.

❧

As they walked back to the meetinghouse after dinner, Sarah Dudley caught Christine's elbow and leaned close to her.

"The parson seemed quite preoccupied at dinner."

"I expect he was thinking of his sermon," Christine said. "He usually studies during the noon hour." She felt an annoying blush returning to her cheeks. Of course she had noticed that Samuel, in his reverie—whatever the topic—had stared at her while he let his thoughts roam. And her friends assumed they were centered on her. How awkward for the pastor. Jane and Sarah wouldn't gossip about it, though. At least she hoped not.

"Somehow I received a different impression," Sarah said.

"Hush. You mustn't put about such a whisper. It would damage the reverend's reputation horribly."

Sarah squeezed her arm. "Oh, my dear, forgive me. I was only teasing. I do love the pastor. We all do. And we've felt so miserable for him this past year. It would cheer us all to think he might be ready to. . ."

"Don't even think it!" Christine glanced quickly about to be sure none of the others had heard. "Sarah, please. It would be painful for me and for Samuel if you entertained such ideas."

"Oh, for *Samuel*." Sarah smiled. "Very well, I shall be quiet. But you must come and see me on a weekday, when there are no listening ears about, and tell me straight to my face that you have not thought of this."

"I don't know what you are talking about."

Sarah stared at her in mock horror with innocent blue eyes. "My dear Christine! I've never known you to lie before, and on the Sabbath!"

Christine's face went scarlet, she was sure, as she passed through the portal of the meetinghouse and into the welcome shadow of the pew.

The opening prayer gave her twenty minutes to calm herself and turn her thoughts heavenward. This was followed by the singing of a psalm. When Samuel at last began to preach, she found her mind riveted to his words.

"Our God is a God of great mercy." Samuel's text was 2 Samuel 24:14. "And David said unto Gad, I am in a great strait: let us fall now into the hand of the Lord; for his mercies are great: and let me not fall into the hand of man." Samuel pleaded earnestly with his congregation to exercise God's mercy toward one another and to all creatures.

Christine felt a tight kink in her chest slowly loosen and unknot. Samuel truly did want to see McDowell treated fairly. To see justice done, yes, but not to see punishment meted out where it was not deserved.

As they left the meetinghouse again two hours later, her heart was full. She hoped for a chance to talk to Samuel in more detail about the implications of the scriptures he had expounded.

She passed a small group of men who clustered outside at the bottom of the steps. Roger Ackley was in their midst, and his angry voice came clearly to her.

"I tell you, the parson's too soft on that evil man. He wants us to go easy on the man who murdered my wife!"

❧

Samuel walked to the Heards' garrison in the late afternoon. He could not stop Roger Ackley from spouting hatred among the people, but he could show an example of charity. He'd stopped at his house only long enough to see the children settled under Christine's care for a few more hours. He'd promised her that he would return ere nightfall and left again carrying a couple of her soft, light biscuits wrapped in a scrap of linen and a pair of his own clean stockings. Let it not be said that he hadn't been evenhanded in his sermons this day.

Justice in the morning, mercy in the afternoon. Surely none could find fault with that.

Yet Roger Ackley did.

Samuel petitioned God for wisdom and entered the gate at the garrison. "Is the prisoner still in the smokehouse?" he asked William Heard's son, Jacob, who met him in the fenced yard. His voice was hoarse from speaking most of the day.

"Aye. We just took him his supper."

"Ah. I should like a word with him."

Jacob led him to the small building between the barn and the woodshed.

McDowell sat with his back against the wall, with an empty pewter plate on his lap and a corked jug beside him. His feet were fettered, though where Goodman Heard had come up with the irons Samuel couldn't imagine. He'd never seen a man chained in Cochecho before. Perhaps Captain Baldwin had supplied them, or maybe the blacksmith had made them specially for this man. Another chain, stout enough to hold a yearling calf, ran from the anklet to a ring in the wall. The man's shoulders slumped, and his spine curved in dejection, his chin resting against his chest until he raised it to see who might be opening the door of his cell.

Samuel thanked Jacob and stepped in. The confined space smelled of bacon and wood smoke and unwashed humanity. He remembered Christine saying the prisoner ought to be allowed to wash. Had they offered him a basin of water, soap, and a towel? "Good evening," he said.

McDowell shifted, and Samuel saw that his hands were linked, too, but with a chain at least two feet long so that he could move them about.

"You be the preacher." McDowell's eyes glinted for a moment.

"Aye." Samuel then stood in silence, seeking God's leading in how to proceed.

"Why'd you come? I suppose she told you what I said I'd do if she gave me away." McDowell squeezed back against the wall, as though afraid the enraged father would beat him for the threats he had made against his children.

"She did, if you mean Miss Hardin," Samuel said. "But that is not why I'm here."

"Why are you here then? Come to save me?"

Samuel sat down on the straw opposite the prisoner. The dim light gave him a poor view of McDowell's face, but the man was watching him warily. "I couldn't do that if I wanted to," Samuel said. "Only Jesus Christ has the power to do that."

McDowell looked away and raised his hands, with a clanking of the chains, in a gesture of futility. "I suppose they're going to hang me t'morra. Sent you to tell me to repent."

"I hope you *will* repent. But no one sent me. No one but the Almighty."

"They're saying I killed a woman."

"Yes, they are."

They sat in silence for long time.

"Thought I was in here for thieving," McDowell said at last.

Samuel peered at him. "Only that?"

"When you all came after me, I thought she'd told, and you were going to drive me out of your township." The man ducked his head and changed his position again. "That girl they call Christine—she brought me food, you know."

"I know."

"That weren't stealing. She gave me things."

"Because you threatened her and those she loves."

"Not I."

Samuel stood. It was no use trying to reason with him.

"Wait, Parson!"

He turned back. "Well?"

McDowell raised his hands in supplication. "I never meant it. I only said it so she'd bring me enough victuals to keep me alive, and I wouldn't have to go and rob someone. I were desperate, you know."

"You could have asked the elders of the village for help. You could have come openly to the parsonage when I was at home. I would have given you sustenance."

"We can't undo what is done, now, can we?"

"Nay, we cannot. But you can still have forgiveness. Even the vilest can repent and experience God's mercy."

"I didn't kill no one."

Samuel sighed. *Lord, show me what to do.*

He sat down again. "You say you didn't kill the woman we found murdered."

"Not I." The prisoner's eyes narrowed. "It weren't the homely girl, were it? She treated me nice, mostly. She got mean at the end and said she wouldn't bring me no more. But she'd given me enough to get by on for a week or two."

Samuel stared at him in disbelief. Was it possible he didn't know who the victim was, or was he cleverly seeking to gain Samuel's trust? "Nay, it was not Miss Hardin. But. . ."

"What?" McDowell asked.

"She wasn't nearly so tall as Christine, and she'd darker hair." That at least was true when Mahalia Ackley was younger; he did not mention that her raven hair had lately been cloaked in gray. "She'd been to the trader, and she carried her purchases home. Are you sure you didn't attack her and steal the bundles that she carried?"

"Nay, sir. I'd remember that, surely I would." His furtive, dark eyes skewered Samuel, and his upper lip curled. "Were she pretty?"

Samuel felt ill. He wanted to flee the felon's presence, but he felt the Lord's leading to stay put. "McDowell, you need Christ, whether you killed that woman or nay."

"You think God Almighty would forgive the likes of me?"

"I know He would."

Again they sat without speaking.

Samuel felt drained of energy and emotion. Did he really want the man who had said he would mutilate his precious little daughters to repent? If he were honest, he would have to admit he wanted the man to hang. But would he wish to see even such an evil person condemned for eternity?

thirteen

Three days later, Christine sat at the loom, throwing the shuttle back and forth through the threads of the warp. Ben and John had both hired out to help with the corn harvest at the Gardners', and John was excited to leave that morning with the prospect of earning half a shilling. She had packed lunch for both of them in a tin pail, which John carried, and Ben took a jug of water for them to share. Samuel had seen the boys off and then gone to the meetinghouse, as usual, to study for his next sermon.

Christine went about her tasks methodically, but her thoughts flitted here and there. She knew that later in the day, Samuel would go to the garrison to visit McDowell. He had gone every day since Sunday. He told her almost nothing about these visits, but Abby had confided to her that in the evening, after she had left, when he read scripture to the children, he instructed them to pray for the prisoner.

She kept praying for McDowell as well, though she had not been told to do so. She prayed for his soul and the magistrate's speedy arrival, and she persisted in asking that justice be done.

While the girls sat on the front step—Abby and Constance with their samplers and Ruth with her doll—Christine wove. The length of gray wool grew daily. Most afternoons, she let Abby put in an hour or two. But the cloth must be finished soon so that she would have time to make all of the clothes the men of the family needed before winter. Her hands flew, and in comparison to Abby's pace, Christine produced material at lightning speed.

While she wove, she brooded. She knew she shouldn't do that, but her thoughts drifted often to Samuel and his somber mood. Was he sorrowful because of the evil McDowell had done or because the man would not repent? Or perhaps it was because of her own part in the drama.

Christine wished she knew what she could do to lighten his heart and take things back to where they had been a month ago, before the outlaw first appeared, before she had accommodated his demands, and before Samuel had ever called her "my dear."

That was it, she realized with a start. Not once, but twice, the minister had spoken thus to her, and each time her pulse had raced. She had allowed herself to imagine that he was conscious of his choice of words, not accidentally using in those moments of tension an endearment that he formerly had bestowed on his wife.

Of course, he called his daughters that as well. He might call any female acquaintance "my dear" in a moment of affection or even out of respect, she supposed. Aye, she had heard him call Tabitha "dear lady." So why should she have felt so giddy when he used the term toward her? But she had.

For the last week, he had gone about with a grave face, never laughing and hardly even playing with the children, something he'd always loved to do. It was almost as if they'd regressed to the weeks after Elizabeth died, when Christine feared Samuel's heart would break with sorrow.

She had been at the loom an hour and was beginning to think she should stop and begin supper preparations, when the girls rushed inside.

"Miss Christine, we have company," Abby called.

"Oh?" Christine rose and hurried to the door.

"It's Miss Catherine," Constance said.

Stephen and Richard Dudley's sister was always a welcome guest. Her youth and enthusiasm couldn't help but lift Christine's spirits.

As she and the little girls spilled out onto the doorstone to meet the caller, Christine saw that Ruth had not stood on ceremony but had run to fling herself into Catherine's arms at the edge of the street. Catherine laughed and stooped to hug her, while juggling her parcels.

Christine walked out with the two older girls to meet her and carry Ruth back. "I'm glad to see you, Catherine! Surely you didn't come into town alone?"

"No, Richard was coming on an errand, and I begged him to bring me to see you. Ever since you told me Abigail was learning to weave, I've been meaning to give her this." She held out a wooden frame about a foot square, laced with heavy thread, which Christine recognized at once as a small hand loom.

"Oh, that's perfect for Abby!" Christine took it and placed it in Abby's hands. "You can weave belts and kerchiefs and all sorts of things on this, my love. Not a large piece of cloth, but small lengths big enough for doll clothes, or towels, or. . .well, anything, if you piece them together."

"Yes, I made pockets and dolly skirts and all sorts of things with that when I was your age," Catherine said. "But I never use it now, and I thought perhaps you would like it."

Abby looked up at Christine, her eyebrows raised so high that the skin of her forehead wrinkled like rows in a plowed field.

Christine laughed. "Yes, you may accept it. I doubt your father will object, and if he does, we'll explain that you are merely borrowing the loom."

"Well, you needn't give it back, so far as I'm concerned," Catherine said as they walked toward the house. "When you outgrow it, Abby, you can pass it on to Constance or Ruth. And this"—she patted the basket that hung from her arm— "is our refreshment. Seed cakes and a packet of chocolate. Father bought the chocolate, but mother doesn't like it. She says it is too bitter to drink. She prefers her sassafras or raspberry tea. Anyway, I wanted you to try it."

"Perhaps if we put sugar in it," Christine said with a frown, though she wasn't sure it would be a good use of the little maple sugar in the parsonage pantry.

"Well, I find it tolerable, but Father is the only one at our house who really likes it," Catherine said. "We'll have fresh cider in another month, and glad we'll be to get it again."

Christine arranged a chair near the doorway for her guest so that Catherine would not get too warm when she stirred up the coals in the hearth to heat their tea water. They spent a pleasant hour talking while Catherine showed Abby how best to thread the hand loom and Christine stirred up fresh biscuits for supper. She hadn't felt like laughing much lately, Christine noted. But with her young guest in the house, merriment was inevitable. She even found herself humming a psalm as she stoked the fire, although perspiration dripped from her brow onto the hearth.

When they'd shared their cakes and chocolate—which they all agreed was better with a scant spoonful of sugar in it—they went to the garden and picked a few carrots, which Christine sliced and added to the stewpot. By the time Richard Dudley came to collect his sister, she realized that Samuel would soon be home for supper. He'd no doubt taken his journey to visit the prisoner, and she hadn't thought about either of them for quite some time. With a guilty start, she sent up a quick, silent prayer as she waved good-bye to Catherine and Richard then herded the Jewett girls back inside to set the table.

❧

Samuel returned home for dinner on Thursday. His sons were both at home that day, as a light rain that morning had put a stop to all harvest activity.

"You boys come over to the meetinghouse with me for an hour after dinner," he said. "I fear you'll forget your Greek and mathematics if we don't continue lessons soon."

"Do you plan to visit the prisoner today?" Christine asked.

He looked at her in surprise. She had not mentioned McDowell for several days, and he'd hoped her preoccupation with him had lessened. "Why, yes. Probably a brief call, after the boys do their sums and grammar. I'll want to study a bit more before evening worship."

"Might I go with you, sir?" Christine's eyelashes stayed low over her expressive eyes, and he couldn't tell from her carefully neutral voice what her mood was.

He hesitated. McDowell was still chained, so she would be in no danger if she kept her distance. William Heard saw to it that he was washed and properly clothed. But still. . .

If he denied her this, would she resent him? And would she find a way to see McDowell without him? Better to take her there himself, he decided. Perhaps if he witnessed the meeting, he would better understand her feelings for the man.

"Shall you come to the meetinghouse in one hour? I'll send Ben home to mind the girls then. Or you could ask Goody Deane to come over for a bit."

"Thank you, sir." She did not smile, nor did she look at him, but went about gathering up the dirty dishes.

She arrived punctually an hour later with a basket on her arm. He had expected that and made no comment. Goody Deane was at the house, she reported, and since the rain had stopped, he allowed the boys to go to the river and fish until suppertime.

The gate stood open at the Heards' garrison, and the men were preparing to go into the fields. William greeted them, eyeing Christine in surprise.

"My wife be inside, making jelly," he told her.

"I shall be glad to see Mrs. Heard," Christine said, "but my real errand is to visit the prisoner."

"The lady comes on an errand of compassion?" Heard asked Samuel. "Well, go along then, but my advice to you is that you go in first and make sure the prisoner is presentable before you admit the lady. He's a hard'un, miss, though lately he's seemed less surly."

"I believe his attitude has changed," Samuel murmured.

Heard nodded. "Well, please do bar the door of the smoke-house from the outside, as usual, when you leave, Parson. I like to think he's secure here, though we haven't posted a guard these past two days."

Samuel followed his suggestion and left Christine outside while he entered the small, dim building.

"Well, Parson"—McDowell sat up straighter on the straw with a crooked smile—"I wondered if you'd forgot me today."

"On the contrary, I've brought someone with me."

"Oh?" The outlaw cocked an eyebrow at him. "Be the magistrate come then?"

"Nay, not yet. This is someone from the village. Someone you've met before."

"Wh—" McDowell peered toward the open door. "Not the girl."

Samuel was glad he hadn't said "the homely girl," for he was certain Christine could hear every word.

"Aye, it's Miss Hardin. She requested to see you."

"Well, now." He smiled and put one hand up to his beard. "I don't make much of a sight for young ladies." His expression changed to a frown. "She don't be come to spit on me and rail at me, does she?"

"Nay, I assure you she would not do so."

"Good. 'Cause that man who came t'other night, I thought he'd kill me. The master had to throw him out of the stockade."

"What man?" Samuel asked.

"They told me it was the husband of her what was killed."

"Roger Ackley was here?"

"That's the name. He ranted and shrieked like a savage. Said they'd ought to string me up. Heard said he'd been hitting the rum, but it gave me a start, I'll tell you."

"Well, you needn't fear a mob coming after you. William Heard and his sons would prevent it, and if need, we would protect you—the captain, Constable Paine, and I, and several other members of my flock. But I shall go and see Roger Ackley and make sure he doesn't do that again. He is distraught, of course."

McDowell shrugged. "I might be guilty of some things, sir, but I should hate awfully to be strung up for something I didn't do."

"I knew it." The doorway darkened, and Christine stood there, her dark skirts blocking much of the sunlight. "Pardon me, but I couldn't help overhearing. I've told the Reverend Jewett several times that you could not have done such a deed."

"There now, miss." McDowell lowered his hands as though to conceal the chains and smiled up at her. "Think of it! Ye've come to see me, after I treated you so mean and all."

"I've forgiven you for that. I wanted to see you for myself and make sure you were well. You must pay for your crimes, sir, I don't deny that, but you must not be made to pay for those someone else committed."

McDowell looked up at Samuel. "Here now, Parson, mayhap

I should have this young lady represent me at court."

Samuel did not find the suggestion amusing. "We must not stay long. Christine, say what you wish, and I shall see you home."

She knelt in the straw before he realized what she was doing and pulled the napkin off her basket.

"Here, I've brought you some biscuits and baked fish. I know they are feeding you, but I thought a bite or two extra would not be amiss. And I've brought ink and paper. I wondered if you wished a letter written to anyone. Do you have family you'd like to notify, sir?"

McDowell blinked and looked up at the pastor with a baffled expression. "Nay, who would I send a letter to? I've never thought of such a thing in my life."

"Well, that's fine," said Samuel. "I'm sure Miss Hardin means well."

"I do," she said. "I tried to think if there was any service you might need while you are here."

McDowell sighed. "Nay, but thank ye kindly, miss. And if you'll allow it before you go, I'd like the parson to pray for me again."

"Of course." She looked up at Samuel, her eyes wide now and shining in the reflected light that streamed through the doorway. She sat back a little away from McDowell.

Samuel bent his knees and lowered himself to the floor. "Shall we pray, then?" The three bowed their heads, and he offered a plea for a swift and just end to McDowell's confinement.

At his amen, the prisoner began a faltering petition. Samuel was not shocked, but he heard Christine's sharp intake of breath.

"God above, look down on this sinner," McDowell said. "Deliver me from my sin, Lord. I do not ask You to deliver me from my bonds, for they are just. Amen."

When he finished, Samuel rose and held out his hand to Christine. She took it and let him pull her to her feet. She sniffed and turned to the prisoner.

"Good day, sir. I shall continue to pray for you daily."

"Thank ye, miss. And you, sir."

Samuel nodded. "Shall we go?" He hopped down the high step to the ground and offered his hand to Christine again. When she stood on the ground beside him, he carefully swung the door shut and put the bars in place.

"Do you wish to see Mrs. Heard now?" he asked.

Christine was patting her cheeks with a handkerchief. "I don't feel like visiting, if the truth be told, but we told her husband I would, so I must."

They paid a brief call at the door of the house, declining to go inside, then set out for the parsonage.

They were halfway there before she spoke. "Does Mr. McDowell pray with you every day when you go to him?"

"Aye. Since Sunday. I believe he truly repented then and came to the cross."

She inhaled deeply. "I'm glad. Thank you for letting me see him."

"Perhaps I should have told you, but. . ." Samuel eyed her carefully. "I did not want you to think I believe him totally innocent."

"Nay, he has admitted he is not. Of the murder only he claims to have a clear conscience."

"Yes, he's confessed other things to me."

She looked up at him, her brows furrowed. "What sort of things? Stealing from us?"

"From us and other people. Dan Otis's knife, Brother Heard's shirt, Goody Deane's loaf of bread. Other things, here and in other villages. Christine, you would not be safe around that man."

"But if he's repented. . ."

Samuel sighed. "Yes. And I believe he means it. But I would want him watched, if he were set free, and made accountable. Sincerity must be proven."

She considered that for a minute as they walked along and then nodded. "What you say is true. If John stole an apple tart and then said he was sorry, I should always watch him on days when I baked."

"Exactly." They went on together, and Samuel felt they were more in tune than they had been all week.

When they were within sight of the meetinghouse, she spoke again. "I understand your concerns, Samuel. McDowell did frighten me, and I'm not sure I'm over that yet. I did see his quick temper and a threatening side to him that I'll not soon forget. But I'm willing to believe he can change, or rather, that God can change him. Still, I don't say he has changed. You're right about that. Time will show whether or not he is the same man who threatened me."

Samuel paused and looked down at her. "I'm glad to hear you say it. I was surprised that you could feel such sympathy for him. For any man, for that matter. You always seemed to distrust men and to avoid them."

"So I did." She hesitated then added, "If it is not too forward, I should like to tell you that I credit your teaching with my change in attitude."

"My. . . You mean from the pulpit?"

"Aye, sir, and in your daily life. You have shown me that we must be open and willing to forgive."

Samuel spotted a cart coming up the street and a man heading toward the ordinary. "Let us walk," he murmured. He must take care still of the village gossips and not be seen lingering with a single woman. "I am glad the Lord has used me to help you."

She nodded but did not look at him as she continued. "I've seen several examples here—the Dudley men, Charles Gardner, indeed, your own example, sir. These godly examples have shown me that some men are kind and trustworthy."

Samuel felt a surge of satisfaction rush over him, followed by a knowledge of his own unworthiness. They reached the doorstone of the parsonage. He glanced about, saw no one watching, and reached for her hand, giving it a quick squeeze and releasing it. "Thank you for sharing that with me. I take it as a deep compliment that you would trust me with your thoughts and that you consider me an example to follow."

She swallowed hard and looked up at him, then away. "Feelings. . .they are so difficult to manage and to share. But they come from above, I am sure."

"Aye." He smiled, knowing he would pray that God would continue to bridge the gap between them. "I shall leave you here now and go back to my studies, though not for long." He looked up at the sun and saw that their trip had taken longer than he'd estimated.

"When do you want supper, sir?"

"I shall return in an hour."

He turned away, but he felt her watching him.

Thank You, Father, for this time together and this new understanding between us. Move us onward, if it be in Your plan, to a sweeter bond.

When he was halfway up the short path to the meeting-house, he turned and looked back. She still stood outside the door. He raised one hand, and she waved back.

fourteen

On Saturday morning, Christine and Goody Deane both went to the parsonage. The elder woman was remaking one of the late Mrs. Jewett's dresses for Abby, and she offered to watch Ruth and sew while Christine and the older children joined the pastor in harvesting the rest of their corn.

As they husked the two bushels of ears they'd picked, dropping the shucks on a pile at the edge of the garden plot, Roger Ackley hobbled into the yard and hailed the pastor.

Samuel walked toward him, meeting him just a few feet from where they worked, and Christine could hear their conversation, whether she wished to or not.

"Brother Ackley," Samuel said. "What brings you out, sir?"

Christine hoped he wasn't here to insist that McDowell should be hung or to blame Samuel for the magistrate's delay. She nodded at Ackley but kept her head down after that, not looking his way but concentrating on her ear of corn.

"I've come to ask you to read banns for me on the Sabbath, sir. And to perform a ceremony three weeks hence."

Startled, Christine looked up. John, Ben, and Abby openly gaped at the man, though Constance appeared not to have noticed what he said and tugged tenaciously at the husks on her ear.

Samuel cleared his throat. "Am I to understand, sir, that you wish to marry again so soon?"

"That I do. You know the Lord says it ain't fittin' that a man should be alone. Now that's scripture." Ackley nodded emphatically.

Christine felt the color rise in her cheeks. She took Constance's ear of corn, quickly finished husking it, and laid it in the basket. "Are you finished?" she asked the other children. "I think we should go inside."

But they did not leave soon enough for her to miss the revelation of the intended bride's name.

"Alice's father won't let her come work for me anymore without I marry her," Ackley explained to the pastor. "And so I says to him, why not? Three weeks from Sunday is the day they chose for the weddin'."

By this time, Christine's ears pulsed with the infusion of blood, and she hustled the girls up the steps, embarrassed on Samuel's account as well as her own.

"Who's out there?" Tabitha Deane asked, laying aside her sewing.

"It's Goodman Ackley." Christine set the basket of corn on the table. "There, we shall have a good feed of roasting ears tonight."

"He wants to marry that hired girl," Ben said, shaking his head.

"Who? Alice Stevens?" Tabitha asked.

"Aye," Christine said.

"Ha!" Tabitha puffed out her breath. "Marry in haste, repent at leisure."

"Is that in the Bible?" Abby asked.

"Nay, but it should be."

"Come, Abby," Christine said. "Fill this kettle with water. John, you and Ben may bring in some more wood, if you please."

A few minutes later, the pastor entered the room. "Well, I seem to be performing another wedding."

"The children told me," Goody Deane said. "That pair seems rather mismatched to me, sir."

Samuel leaned against the mantel. "I told Ackley I will visit the girl at her parents' home and speak to all three. I've seen stranger things."

"She's not yet twenty, is she?"

"I'm not sure."

"Well, Roger Ackley be well past fifty." Tabitha shook her head.

"He should marry you, Goody Deane," said Constance.

"Ha! That's clever. You think I would wed that man?"

"Well now, perhaps we'd best turn the topic here," Samuel said gently. "All I know is that Goodman Ackley says he needs Alice to cook for the men he'll hire at harvest, and she can't stay at the farm to work unless they are wed."

"But that's—" Christine stopped and swallowed her words. It was not her place to object.

By evening, the pastor had made his trip to the Stevens house and returned. He said nothing while the children were about, but when Christine had hung up her apron and prepared to leave, he bid her wait and he would accompany her.

Her pulse beat quicker as she waited for him to don his hat and jacket.

"Children, I shall return in a trice," he called.

Christine felt a foolish smile tugging at the corners of her mouth as they stepped onto the path together.

"I would say you needn't escort me home, but I know it wouldn't change your mind."

"You are correct in that. I find it gives me a chance to speak privately with you. Do you mind?"

"Not at all."

"Christine, this precipitous marriage of Ackley's does concern me, but I find no grounds to refuse to perform the ceremony. The girl told me to my face she is agreeable, though she knows it to be a marriage of convenience for Ackley. Of course, it will elevate her status in the community. Ackley is better off than her own father, who is a mere laborer in the brickworks. But her parents seem to have no objection. Her mother even offered to go with her to the farm next week to help her cook for his harvesting crew."

"That was good of her," Christine said.

He frowned and shook his head slightly. "I asked her mother if she'd talked to Alice and explained what marriage would mean, and she said she was sure the girl would be fine." He glanced at her and halted, a few yards from Tabitha's door. "I'm sorry, Christine. I shouldn't burden you with this."

"Think nothing of it. You need someone to express your reservations to."

"Nay, I should take them to the Lord. But. . .I do enjoy talking to you. I've had no one to discuss such things with since. . ." He pressed his lips together.

Christine's heart wrenched. He missed Elizabeth, of course. And she was a poor substitute. "Well, sir, I do not mind if you speak to me about your concerns, and you can be sure that what you say will go no further."

"Thank you." He took her hand once again and held it. Her heart pounded. "Christine, your friendship means a great deal to me."

"And yours to me." She looked down at their clasped hands and took a careful breath. Could this really be happening?

"I expect that when I read the banns tomorrow, all the girls will gather around Alice and congratulate her, and yet. . . something about it bothers me." He seemed to realize suddenly that he still held her hand in his. He squeezed it gently and released it. "Forgive me. I presume too much."

"Do you, sir?" she whispered.

His eyes flashed with something—what? He drew in a

breath and looked away. "I do understand a man. . .a widower. . . wishing to remarry."

She found it impossible to inhale. After a long pause, she squeaked out, "Do you?"

"Aye." They looked at each other. "Christine. . ." Samuel raised his hand and halted with it in midair, as though debating which to touch—her hair or her face. She thought her heart might burst if he did neither.

Behind her, Goody Deane's door creaked open. Samuel quickly stepped back a pace.

Tabitha chuckled. "I may be old, but I'm not blind. Don't you think it's time you began calling on this young woman?"

&

The reaction to Sunday's public reading of the banns set Christine's sympathy for Samuel soaring, but she could not show it. The congregants gasped as one when the pastor read the names on the marriage intentions. Samuel spent the noon hour closeted in the meetinghouse with his deacons. When he emerged, there was no time for him to eat dinner, and Christine was able only to slip him a cup of cider and a slice of journey cake.

"Is all well, Samuel?" she whispered.

"Aye, and thank you, my dear." He pressed the empty cup back into her hand. His afternoon sermon, if anything, was more lucid and elegant than the morning's. Christine drank in every word. It was the one time she could stare her fill at him without arousing suspicion, and she took full advantage of it that day.

Once, when he called them all to join him in prayer, she noticed Samuel's gaze resting on her before he shut his eyes. Just for that instant, she felt his warmth and affection. She was glad all eyes were closed then and that she had the high wall of the pew at her back.

That night, he again walked her home from the parsonage after supper was over, but this time Goody Deane was with them.

"Some of the elders wondered if there shouldn't be a waiting period for remarriage after the death of a spouse," he told them.

"I never heard anything like it," Tabitha said.

"Nor I. And I've seen a woman who was with child married a week after her husband was killed by a bull. I suppose I could refuse to solemnize the vows, but to what end?"

❧

Nearly the entire village turned out Monday morning for the hearing at the meetinghouse. Catherine Dudley and Tabitha kept the children of several families at the parsonage with the young Jewetts.

Christine put on her Sunday best and went with the pastor, in expectation of being called upon to testify. She slid into the customary pew and felt people staring as Samuel joined her. The pastor had never sat in the pew before, to her knowledge. Certainly never beside her. The scrutiny of the villagers set her nerves on edge. Her hands trembled as she arranged her skirts.

McDowell was brought in and made to sit in the elders' pew between Baldwin and Paine, his wrists and ankles still chained. He stared down at the floor. A stranger in a cutaway coat and breeches sat near him, and Christine looked to Samuel and arched her brows.

"The lawyer," Samuel whispered. "I fear the crown must pay for his services, which means we shall be taxed for them."

The men had placed a table at the front, on the platform with the pulpit. The bewigged magistrate entered with great pomp and took his seat behind it.

When Christine was called to face the magistrate, she took

her place knowing every eye was upon her. Her voice shook as she recounted how McDowell had accosted her again and again, demanding food and other comforts.

"And did the accused ever harm you physically?" the magistrate asked.

"Nay, he never laid hands on me."

"Did he threaten you bodily harm?"

"Not I, sir, but others. He told me that if I did not do as he wished, he would hurt others who were close to me."

"And who would that be?"

She inhaled and glanced toward Samuel. His compassionate blue eyes looked back at her, and he nodded almost imperceptibly.

"The parson's children, sir." A sympathetic murmur went up from the congregation. "I be in charge of them most days, for the Reverend Jewett."

"And the accused said he would hurt them?"

"Aye. He showed me a knife the first time, and one other time. And more than once, he said he would hurt them. He said. . ." She shuddered, recalling his words. "Despicable things, sir. I do not wish to repeat them before the children's father."

Samuel's head drooped, and she thought she could see the sheen of tears in his eyes. A whisper rippled through the ranks of the people. The magistrate hit his gavel on the table and bid her step down.

Others went forward and told about the thefts they had experienced, and one farmer told how his dog had chased a man off one night, but he hadn't gotten a good look at the intruder. Captain Baldwin described the search for Mahalia Ackley, and at last the pastor gave his tale of the finding of McDowell in the thicket.

The magistrate recessed the hearing and went to the

ordinary for his dinner. Meanwhile, the people either went to their homes or milled about the common, eating the refreshments they had brought and discussing the testimony.

Samuel and Christine walked back to the parsonage together.

"I'm sorry you had to go through this," he said on the way.

"It is needful."

The house was full of children. Samuel cast a woebegone look at Christine, retreated into his bedchamber, and closed the door. She waited while Tabitha fixed a plate and a cup of strong tea for him, then she took it to the door. When she knocked on the panel, he opened it a crack.

"You must eat, sir," Christine said.

"Thank you. I don't feel hungry, but I suppose I must." He took the plate and cup then looked earnestly into her eyes. "This will be over soon."

"Yes. Pray for justice."

fifteen

That afternoon, the hearing was reconvened. The magistrate asked McDowell if he wished to speak on his own behalf.

McDowell shuffled to the witness chair and took the oath to speak the truth.

"Tell us, then," the magistrate said, looking him over with narrowed eyes. "Did you commit the heinous acts described here this morning?"

"Aye, sir, all but one."

The people burst out in exclamations of surprise, and the magistrate banged on the table. "Silence." He fixed his gaze on McDowell, still scowling. "Make yourself clear, sir."

McDowell's attorney rose. "Your honor, the prisoner admits his guilt to the petty thefts previously alluded to and to intimidating Miss Hardin and threatening the children. However, he maintains he did not kill the aforementioned Mahalia Ackley." He sat down with a self-satisfied expression.

The magistrate tapped his gavel on the table once more. "The court finds there is enough evidence to hold the prisoner, Abijah McDowell, for trial. He is to be held locked up where he was housed heretofore until the trial. The Lord willing, I shall return here in a fortnight to carry out that business. Meanwhile, the prisoner's attorney will prepare his case."

The lawyer nodded, and the judge dismissed the hearing.

Christine stood, feeling a bit let down. "Seems nothing has changed," she said to Samuel.

"Aye. Another two weeks." The creases at the corners of his eyes looked deeper, and his eyes duller.

"You need rest, sir," Christine said softly.

"As do you. Come. Let us go home."

As they made their way out, they passed the attorney, who was speaking to the owner of the ordinary. "It sounds as though I shall have to lie over tonight at your establishment, sir. I regret I must remain here even another day."

" 'Tis not so unpleasant a place, sir," said the innkeeper.

"Nay, but I'll lose business I could be doing in Portsmouth for better pay than I shall receive for this, I'll tell you."

As Christine and Samuel walked toward the parsonage, they met several couples who had been to retrieve their children from Tabitha and Catherine's care. When they arrived, all of the children had left except the Jewett brood and Charles and Jane Gardner's little boy.

"I'll carry little Johnny over to the common," Catherine offered. "I expect Jane and Charles tarried there to talk to people."

She bid them good-bye and left with the baby and a bundle of his things.

John Jewett went to stand before his father. "Be they going to hang that man?"

"I don't know, son. Today was not the trial but merely a hearing to see if the case warrants a trial. The judge will return a fortnight hence, and the matter will be settled then."

"May we go next time?" Ben asked.

Samuel sighed. "I hardly think I want my children to attend such a proceeding."

Tabitha said sharply, "You young'uns clear out now. You can see your father's tired. Let him rest while Miss Christine and I get supper on."

"No, really." Samuel held up both hands and looked around at his offspring. "I believe I'd rather sit out under the oak tree with the children for a while. It does my heart good to see them around me, all strong and healthy."

Christine touched his arm. "Then you do that, sir. We'll bring you some refreshment out yonder."

She watched the children, quieted by their father's un-accustomed manner, surround him and head for the door. Ruth and Constance took his hands and pulled him along.

"That man is exhausted," said Tabitha.

"Aye." Christine reached for her apron. "Let me take him some cider, and then I'll get on a large supper for them all. You must be tired, too. Why don't you go home and lie down?"

"I'll help you. Then we shall both go home and leave them in peace for the evening."

Christine eyed her for a moment then put her hands on Goody Deane's shoulders and stooped to kiss the old woman's wrinkled cheek. "Thank you, dear lady. You are a blessing."

Tabitha waved her comment aside. "This will cheer you. This morning, Mrs. Gardner brought a haunch of venison, or rather, her husband did. And Mrs. Leeds, when she brought her three children, left a blackberry pudding. I made sure to put it up where the young'uns wouldn't get into it."

Christine gave her a weary smile. "Then let's get at it. The Jewett children and their father will feast tonight."

⊰⊱

The next morning, Christine took the three Jewett girls with her to the trading post. Samuel had taken the boys with him to the meetinghouse for lessons, and Tabitha had stayed at home to do her own washing and light cleaning.

Christine disliked going to the trader's, but sometimes it was necessary, and she found that they needed some hooks and eyes for Abby's new Sunday dress and a few stores for the parsonage larder. Samuel had entrusted her with two shillings that morning, and she feared it might be the last of his silver.

She and the girls entered and went to the counter where sewing notions were displayed. She was surprised to see Alice Stevens there as well, fingering rolls of braid. "Good day, Alice," she said.

"Hello." Alice seemed distracted as she compared the selection of fripperies.

"Good day, Miss Stevens." Abby dropped a pretty curtsy, and Christine felt a stab of pride. The eight-year-old's manners were better than many adults'.

Alice shot her a smile that was almost a smirk. "Soon-to-be Goody Ackley." She held out a roll of fancy black braid so Christine could see it. "The master—that is, my soon-to-be husband—has given me his late wife's clothing. I intend to cut down her somber old dresses and fix them up with pretty trimmings. Think you this would look well on her plum-colored wool?"

Christine gulped for air. "I'm sure I don't know. I'm. . .not one who knows much about fashion."

Alice looked her over for a second. "Aye, so you don't." She turned back to her shopping.

Christine inhaled slowly, feeling the flush creep up her neck. Abby's look of distress prodded her to control herself.

"Come, girls, let us find the hooks we need."

A few minutes later, they were outside the trading post and headed for home. Christine picked Ruth up to carry her and let Abby tote their small purchases in her basket.

"Miss Christine," Constance said, looking up at her soberly and clutching her free hand, "did she rude us?"

❧

Elder Heard blew the conch shell Sunday morning, and all the villagers hastened toward the meetinghouse. The temperatures had moderated, with a promise of autumn on the breeze, and all of the women donned shawls that morning.

As they reached the common before the meetinghouse, Christine spotted Alice Stevens approaching in the company of her parents. It did not surprise her that Alice wore her late mistress's plum-colored wool skirt and bodice or that the skirt was edged in swoops of black braid. She tried to forget the impolite words the young woman had spoken at the trader's. Alice's coming marriage seemed to have altered her attitude toward her neighbors. Christine hoped it was not a permanent change.

Jane Gardner hurried toward her with little Johnny on her hip. "Christine! Good day."

Christine smiled. "Ah, well met, Jane."

"What were you staring at?" Jane threw a quick look over her shoulder at the people entering the meetinghouse.

Christine ducked her head. "I'm embarrassed to say it, but I was surveying the future Goody Ackley's fashions."

Jane squinted toward the church steps. "Ah, a new gown?"

"New to the wearer. I met her at the trader's Tuesday, and she was buying trimmings for the late Goody Ackley's old clothing."

Jane nodded with comprehension. "Ah. It seems she has also acquired the mistress's fine scarf from England. Remember how Mahalia used to wear it to meeting?"

"Every Sunday," Christine agreed.

"Well, ladies."

Christine jumped at the pastor's voice. She'd thought him inside long ago.

"Good day, Pastor," Jane said with a smile. "Oh, here comes my husband. Pardon me." She hastened toward Charles.

"Surely you ladies weren't lingering to gossip this fine Sabbath morning?" Samuel arched his eyebrows.

"Certainly not, sir." Christine clamped her lips together.

All through the worship service, the scene replayed in her

mind. By the end of the final psalm, she wallowed in guilt so low that she doubted she would ever leave the morass.

She took the children home and set out their dinner. She left them setting the table and ran out to see if the pastor was headed home. He came from the church, and she met him a short distance from the house. "Forgive me, sir, but I had to speak to you in private. You hit the mark this morning. My behavior was unconscionable."

Samuel eyed her keenly. "If you've aught to regret, Christine, I'm not your confessor. Take it to the Lord."

"Aye, and I have, to be sure. But I wish your pardon as well. For I not only gossiped with Jane, but I lied to you about it." Her voice quivered. "I wouldn't have thought I could do that, but it slipped out so easily!"

"This. . .gossip. Will it hurt the person in question?"

"I don't know, sir. I doubt it. But it has hurt me. It's made me see myself as mean-spirited, a character trait I do not wish to possess. Why should I care if Alice's affianced husband gives her his dead wife's skirts and English scarf? But I don't wish to be an example to your children of a petty, shrewish woman."

"Did the children overhear?"

She hung her head. "I don't think so. And when we saw Alice at the trader's, I believe I accepted her scorn without giving a poor example to the girls."

"Alice scorned you?"

She felt flames in her cheeks. "It is nothing, sir. What she spoke was true, but perhaps said unkindly."

"The same as what you did this morning, then, only to your face?"

"Aye."

He nodded. "My dear, I admire your tender conscience. Would that all my parishioners had such."

"Oh, Samuel, I promise you that with God's help I shall endeavor not to speak ill of others or to be uncharitable."

Samuel sighed. "Perhaps the Almighty had a purpose in your exchange with Goody Gardner."

"Oh?" She blinked and waited for him to speak further.

"Your talk this morning drew my attention to the scarf Alice Stevens wore."

Christine was baffled. "And?"

"And I recalled that Goody Ackley nearly always wore it when going out in public, as you say. That is all."

Christine squinted at him against the sun, feeling certain that, on the contrary, that was not all.

sixteen

In the week before the trial, the nights turned chilly. Samuel spent much time in the fields, getting in his crops and helping the men of his parish harvest their grain and flax.

At last the magistrate and lawyer returned, along with a second attorney to represent the crown. The people gathered once more at the meetinghouse. Christine wished she could sit at the back of the room, but as witnesses, she and Samuel were bid to sit in the usual pew occupied by the pastor's family, along with Charles Gardner, who brought his wife this time. Samuel also allowed Ben and John to join them, and so the pew was nearly filled.

Christine felt quite warm in the close quarters and extremely conscious of Samuel's nearness. From time to time, one of them shifted, bringing their two shoulders into contact. Christine tried to ease away slightly, without drawing attention to the movement, all the while wishing she could relax and rest against Samuel's strong arm.

Goodman Ackley occupied his usual pew, though it was farther back than he would like. Alice, his soon-to-be wife, sat primly beside him, darting glances at the people around them. Her new attire reflected her future elevated status as the wife of a fairly prosperous farmer rather than that of a hired girl.

Christine was glad that when she had sat down, Alice could not see her. Not many in the congregation could. However, the magistrate, the attorneys, and the prisoner, as well as whoever sat on the stool used as a witness stand, had a first-rate view of her and the minister. She determined to stay alert and not give one tiny crumb of behavior that could be used to criticize Samuel.

She looked past Ben at Jane Gardner, and Jane gave her a feeble smile. The solemnity of the occasion was overpowering. Christine wondered if it would be better for her to sit on the other side of Jane, not beside Samuel. His proximity continually drew her thoughts to him, which might cause her to look at him often, which in turn might lead others to think malicious thoughts.

Joseph Paine, the trader who doubled as constable, stood and called the session to order. Much of the testimony seemed repetitious to Christine. She recounted the same facts she'd given at the hearing, and she couldn't see that the other witnesses added much to their previous information, until the crown's attorney brought forth the market basket Stephen Dudley had found in the woods.

Seventeen-year-old Stephen was called to tell how he discovered the item and where and when. "No more questions," said the lawyer.

"But it wasn't there a day earlier," Stephen said.

"No more questions," repeated the lawyer.

The magistrate looked at McDowell's attorney. "Your witness, sir."

The defense attorney rose, his eyes gleaming. "Now, Master Dudley, you said you found this basket near the camp in the thicket. That would be the same camp you and your brother found the day after the accused was arrested."

"Aye, sir."

"So you were there on the Friday with your brother."

"I was, sir."

"And you found no basket then."

"We did not. Richard can tell you, sir."

"Oh, we shall get to your brother, have no fear. Yet you say that on the Saturday morning, the basket lay there, on the ground, in plain sight."

"Exactly so, sir."

Christine was proud of the boy's calmness.

"How do you explain that, Master Dudley?"

"I don't, sir."

"So when you found this basket, on the Saturday morning, what did you do with it?"

"I took it along to the parsonage. I thought to ask the constable or the pastor about it."

"And what did they say?"

"They weren't t'home, sir. Both had gone to Portsmouth to ask for you and his honor to come."

"Ah." The attorney nodded in encouragement. "What did you then?"

"Miss Hardin said she would go with me to Goodman Ackley's to ask if it were his wife's basket, and I said mayhap we should get the captain to go, too. So I fetched Captain Baldwin and we went."

"And what happened at the Ackleys' farm?"

"The master and Alice Stevens, what were the hired girl, both said it were Goody Ackley's basket."

Richard Dudley and Captain Baldwin were summoned to the stand in turn, and both confirmed Stephen's testimony.

Goodman Ackley was next. In mournful tones, he told how his wife had gone off that morning and how he regretted not accompanying her on her errand. The crown's attorney asked if she had carried the basket previously introduced as evidence, and he declared that she had.

Alice Stevens was called next. She swayed down the aisle in her finery, took the oath, and sat down on the stool. Like her affianced former master, she bewailed the goodwife's disappearance and death, and she stated that Mahalia Ackley had indeed carried her customary basket that day.

The magistrate declared a recess at that point, and Christine and the Jewetts walked home for lunch, taking the Gardners with them. Samuel seemed preoccupied, but he joined in conversation with the guests and Tabitha while they sat at dinner.

As they left the parsonage to return to the trial, he murmured to Christine, "Forgive me if I hasten on ahead. I must have a word with the defense attorney before court reconvenes."

She watched him hurry off, surprised at his agitation.

"The parson's a bit on edge," Charles observed as they followed at a slower pace.

Jane said, "I thought so, too. Both during the testimony this morning and at dinner. Has this business made him restless, Christine?"

"Nay, but we would both like to see it finished well."

"Of course," Charles said. "But is there much doubt of the outcome?"

Christine watched Samuel as he hurried into the meeting-house. Something wasn't right, she thought. Something other than the basket. Samuel must feel it, too.

They filed into the Jewett pew again, and Samuel joined them. His face was sober, but he tossed a faint smile at Christine as he settled beside her.

The boys traipsed in just before Paine stood to call the crowd to order.

Samuel leaned toward her. "Pray, my dear."

Startled, she nodded, unable to look into his face for fear she would betray the mixed apprehension and sweet pleasure his words brought her.

Mrs. Paine, the wife of the trader, was called forward. She

acknowledged that she had waited on Goody Ackley the morning the woman disappeared and recounted the items the customer had purchased and placed in her large basket.

"And that was the basket you saw here this morning?"

"I believe it was, sir."

The crown's attorney then relinquished the floor to the defense council.

"Can you recall what the deceased wore that day?" McDowell's attorney asked.

Mrs. Paine eyed him thoughtfully.

Samuel's hands clenched into fists.

Christine listened carefully as the trader's wife spoke.

"Yes, sir, she wore her gray linsey skirt and a blue bodice over her shift, and of course her bonnet and scarf."

"A shawl, do you mean?" asked the attorney.

"Why, no, sir." Mrs. Paine sat up straighter and looked out over the meetinghouse. "I mean a particular scarf that she always wore into town or to meeting. Her husband had bought it for her at an emporium in Boston a year or two back, and she was very vain of it."

The magistrate tapped his gavel. "Keep your responses to the facts, madam."

"Aye, sir. But she wore it that day, and she often boasted that her husband had paid a great sum for it. Raw silk, she called it. Hmpf. I'm sure it's largely woolen, with perhaps a bit of silk woven in. If you'd like to see it, you've only to cast your eyes o'er the far pew, where the husband of the deceased sits now, with his betrothed and her family. In fact, your honor"—Mrs. Paine turned and gazed up at the magistrate—"Alice Stevens wore it when she sat in this very spot to give testimony this morning, and she wears it still."

A noise of whispering swelled amidst the people.

Again the magistrate clapped his gavel to the desk. "Silence."

The immediate stillness was broken by only the lowing of a cow on the common.

The magistrate studied Mrs. Paine. To the lawyer, he said, "Have you any more questions for this witness, sir?"

"No, your honor."

Mrs. Paine returned to her pew, and the crown rested its case. The defense attorney stood and turned toward the onlookers.

"The defense calls Doctor Elias Cooke, resident of Dover Point."

Samuel inhaled deeply as a man walked quietly up the aisle. The physician wore a powdered wig and a long, black coat and breeches. Christine felt Samuel's tension as Paine administered the oath to the physician, and when she glanced at him, she saw that Samuel's face was pale.

"Doctor Cooke," said the attorney, "you were called to examine Mahalia Ackley's body soon after it was discovered." The attorney stood sideways so that he could look at the witness and also at the onlookers if he wished.

"That is correct, sir."

"Why were you summoned here?"

"They have no physician in Cochecho, and Captain Baldwin asked if I would come and examine a dead woman to tell him what I could."

"And how long after her death did you see her?"

"I believe it was a few hours after death occurred. No greater than eight hours, from what I've heard of her activity that morning."

"And were you able to determine how Mahalia Ackley died?"

The physician looked up at him and said calmly, "Aye, sir. She had a wound on her temple, and her face was bruised, but I believe she was killed by strangling."

"Strangling, you say?"

"Aye. Her throat was marked where something had been pulled tight about it, and the blood vessels in her eyes had ruptured."

"And could you say what instrument was used to kill her?"

The doctor shook his head slightly. "I believe it to have been an article of clothing, sir."

The swell of low voices began again, but when the magistrate lifted his gavel, it subsided.

"A specific article of clothing, sir? For instance, would you say a belt?"

"Nay, not that." The doctor unbuttoned a few silver buttons and reached inside his coat. "The minister assisted me in my examination, and since he is one who often stands in as a healer in this community, I welcomed his aid. I pointed out to him an oddity pertaining to the wounds."

"And what was that, sir?"

"Fibers clinging to the creased skin of the victim's neck." He held out a folded piece of paper. "It may interest you and the magistrate to look at them. The Reverend Jewett"— Cooke nodded in Samuel's direction—"can tell you. He saw me remove several white fibers from the body. I believe the woman was strangled with an article woven of fine white wool and silk."

A shriek came from the rear of the hall. Christine looked at Samuel, but he had already jumped to his feet and turned to look over the back of their pew. Christine leaped up and looked toward the rear of the room.

Alice Stevens clawed the white scarf from about her neck, threw it on the floor, and crumpled into her father's arms.

seventeen

The uproar could not be silenced by the pounding gavel. Paine and Captain Baldwin leaped into the aisles in an attempt to calm the surging crowd.

Christine sat down hard on her wooden seat and shrank back against the pew, thankful she couldn't see what went on behind them but wondering what Alice Stevens and Roger Ackley were doing at that moment. She had an excellent view of McDowell, who craned his neck to see what was happening, grinning as he pulled against the leg irons and fetters that held him to the deacons' pew.

Samuel plopped down beside her and stared straight ahead.

After a good ten minutes, order was restored. The magistrate declared a quarter hour's recess, after which all witnesses were expected to appear ready to testify again if called.

John Jewett was standing on his seat, looking over the high back of the pew. As the crowd began to surge toward the door, he cried, "Father! Alice Stevens swooned. How can she testify again?"

Samuel shook his head. "We shall see, son."

"Her mother and father are trying to rouse her," Jane noted.

Samuel stroked his beard. Christine saw that his hand shook. "Perhaps I should see if they need assistance," he said.

"That doctor's looking at her," Ben reported, also peering over the top of the pew.

Samuel drew a deep breath. "We wished for justice, Christine. Do not cease your praying now." He patted her arm briefly and then clasped his hands in his lap.

"Do you wish to go outside?" Charles asked Jane.

"Mayhap we are better off to stay right here and see what befalls," his wife replied.

Christine was glad. She did not feel like facing the inquisitive stares and questions of the villagers. She sat stiffly beside Samuel, pondering all that she had heard. The two attorneys huddled with the magistrate at the front table. As Samuel had suggested, she leaned back, closed her eyes, and prayed silently.

After ten minutes, Charles left them for a short time and returned with a dipper of cold water, which he offered first to Jane then to Christine.

She took a sip, thankful for the cool liquid.

"Pastor, would you like a drink?" Charles asked.

Samuel took the dipper and drained it. "Thank you, Charles." He slumped back against the wall.

Charles took the dipper away. When he returned, he bent close to Samuel. "Goodman Ackley tried to bolt. Baldwin's got him in custody. They're going to bring him in last, when everyone's seated again."

"What about the scarf?"

"The attorney asked Alice's parents to give it to them as evidence. She's come round, but she still looks like death. They've moved out of Ackley's pew to another at the side."

Soon afterward, court reconvened. The defense attorney called Alice Stevens to the front of the room. Everyone stared at the hired girl as she rose, her face white. Her father escorted her to the witness stand, holding firmly to her elbow.

After she was reminded of her oath to tell the truth, McDowell's attorney directed his questions to her. "Miss Stevens, you were in Goody Ackley's employ at the time of her death?"

"Yes, sir."

"And where did you get the scarf you wore to court today?"

"My. . . Her husband gave it to me, sir."

"Why did he do that?"

Alice hung her head. Her answer was so quiet, Christine could barely hear it. "A week and more after she died, he asked me to be his wife."

"And you accepted?"

"Aye." She looked up quickly. "I thought—" She let out her breath in a puff and blinked as tears flooded her eyes and raced down her cheeks. "He gave me some of her clothing, sir. That were among 'em."

"And can you remember exactly when he gave you that scarf, Miss Stevens?"

She shook her head. "A few days ago, I think."

"Did you see it the day your mistress died?"

"I. . .don't know, sir."

"Did she wear it when she left for the trading post?"

"I'm not sure."

The attorney took a few steps across the front of the meeting-house as though deep in thought and turned to face her again. "Was she wearing it when they brought the body home?"

"Nay. Of that I'm certain, sir."

The men who had discovered the body in the woods off the road to Ackley's farm were called back and asked if the dead woman's scarf was on or near the body when they found it. All said no.

Next, Paine himself testified that Mahalia wore the article in question when she came in to trade on the fateful day. A woman who was in the shop at the time also swore that the deceased had worn the scarf.

Finally, Roger Ackley was called. The congregation hushed as he walked slowly up the aisle beside Captain Baldwin, dragging his feet with each step. He snuffled and took the stand. Again, the magistrate reminded the witness of his oath.

The magistrate fixed his stern gaze on Ackley's face. "Goodman Ackley, what say you? I have examined the fibers Dr. Cooke gathered from your wife's body and found them similar to ones I gleaned from the scarf you presented to Alice Stevens last week. So similar that I would not be loathe to say they came from that scarf. Have you an explanation?"

Ackley opened his mouth then closed it. He looked around, his eyes wild. He started to rise, but Paine and Baldwin, on either side of the stool, pushed him back down. He pulled in a shuddering breath. "My wife wore that scarf often. I gave a pretty price for it, and she doted on it. It is not unnatural that some of the threads should cling to her. . .skin."

The magistrate frowned. "The physician tells me they would not stick as they did from a casual wearing. Sir, your wife was strangled with this garment." He held up the white scarf. "I ask you, sir, where has it been since the day your wife wore it to her death?"

"I do not think she wore it that day, sir. Nay, she can't have. I found it later, among her things."

"As you found her basket?" the attorney asked.

"What. . .I do not understand you, sir."

"Where did you find it?"

"Why. . .in the chest at our home."

"You wife's basket was on her arm when she left the trading post. The scarf was about her neck. Her body was found a few hours later. No basket was present. No scarf. The basket turned up the next day at the outlaw's camp. Yet it was not there when he was captured. The scarf turned up in your wife's clothes chest."

McDowell's attorney swung around and addressed the

magistrate. "Your honor, I submit that my client did not kill Mrs. Ackley. Rather, I ask you to believe the evidence. The poor woman was strangled by her own husband, who placed the basket at McDowell's camp to make him look guilty. But he couldn't bear to discard the scarf he'd paid so much for. Nay, sir. He had his eye already on a younger, fairer woman, and he gave it to her when he wooed her."

The magistrate held up both hands. "Sir, Goodman Roger Ackley is not on trial today. However, I instruct the captain to remand him into custody until a hearing can be held to ascertain whether there be sufficient evidence to pursue this line of inquiry. Meanwhile, the accused, Mr. McDowell, has confessed to several petty crimes." He picked up a piece of parchment and read them off. "I shall recess for one hour, and when we return, I shall pronounce sentence on McDowell for these lesser crimes. I find there is not sufficient evidence to convict said McDowell of murder."

❧

The next morning, Samuel walked to William Heard's garrison in a chilly downpour. Few people were about the roads.

The magistrate and lawyers had spent the night at the ordinary but planned to leave together after they broke their fast. Baldwin had commissioned two men to go with him to deliver McDowell to the jail at Portsmouth.

Samuel felt he needed to see the man once more before he left to fulfill his year's sentence in jail.

William Heard admitted him to the smokehouse. Baldwin was already there, checking the leg irons in preparation to removing the prisoner.

"Thank you for coming, Parson," McDowell said when he saw Samuel.

"I came to see if you needed anything and to tell you that I shall continue to pray for you."

"Thankee, sir. I know I deserve what I'm gettin'. I guess I can stand a year, so long as they don't throw me in a dank, cold hole for the winter."

"I trust they will see to your bodily needs. Do not lose hope, McDowell. Do not lose faith in God Almighty."

"I shan't, sir. He knows I'm sorry I done what I did. And He made it so I shan't be hanged for killing that woman, such as I didn't do."

Samuel nodded and turned to Baldwin. "Captain, this man is a brother in Christ. Please allow us to pray once more before you take him away."

An hour later, Samuel entered his house and removed his dripping hat. Christine was near the hearth, coughing as she stirred a simmering kettle. As much smoke seemed to billow from the fireplace as went up the chimney. The fire sputtered as rain pattered down on it. He looked about, mentally counting the children in the haze, and relaxed when he was sure all were safe within the walls of home.

"Ah, there you be, sir. Your coat at least is soaked, and probably your other clothing as well. You'd best change and hang your things here to dry."

He ducked into his bedchamber and closed the door. On his pallet lay a new suit of charcoal gray wool. He bent and ran his hand over it. So. She had finished her weaving and sewing, despite all that went on in the village.

Well, this suit was too good for him to loll about home in or to wear over to the meetinghouse for school time and preparing sermons. He put on the workaday trousers she had made him that summer and a different shirt. She was right; he'd gotten soaked to the skin.

He carried his wet garments out to hang near the fire. Christine had left the door open, and the smoke had cleared a little.

"Where are the children?" he asked.

"I sent them all to the loft under Ben's direction to crack nuts for me. I am baking a cake."

"I see."

"Do you, sir? Today is your birthday, you know."

That tickled Samuel, and he laughed. "I had forgotten it."

"Well, I had not." She wiped her hands on her apron and opened the crock where she kept pearl ash for her soapmaking.

He heard Abby's clear, ringing laugh and looked up. He could just see her back and Ben's. They were sitting on the floor chattering together while they worked. Despite the rain, despite the bleak events of the last month, he felt happier than he had in a long, long time.

"Christine."

"Aye?"

He stepped toward her and seized her hand. "My dear, you are lovely in your cap, with flour smudged on your nose."

She froze and stared at him.

"It is my hope that in the past two and a half years you've come to think of this cottage as your home."

"Oh, I have, sir," she whispered. She tore her gaze from his and looked down at their clasped hands.

Samuel smiled gently and tipped her chin up until she looked at him again. "It is also my hope that you will consider an offer to make this your permanent home. Christine, if you feel you can find peace here in this house. . ."

"I believe I can."

His smile grew without his trying to restrain it. "And if you can love my children as your own. . ."

"I do so already, sir. You know that."

"Yes, I do. And if you think perchance you might one day love me. . ."

She lowered her lashes. He waited, and after a long moment,

she looked up into his eyes once more. "I do not believe in chance, sir."

He laughed and pulled her to him. "Marry me, then, dear Christine. Soon. I'll ask the minister from Dover Point to read the banns. May I?"

Her glowing smile answered him, although she got no words out before John called down from the loft, "Father! What are you doing?"

epilogue

When the harvest was in and the golden days of October belied the coming bitter winds of winter, the Reverend Samuel Jewett took Christine Hardin as his lawfully wedded wife.

Her friends and the Jewett girls clustered about her. Jane and Sarah helped her dress in a fine new skirt and bodice. Ruth presented a bouquet of dried blossoms she and her sisters had made. The visiting preacher awaited them at the meetinghouse with Samuel and his sons. When they stepped outside for the short walk from the parsonage, Goody Deane hobbled out from her cottage and joined them.

James Dudley's wagon was tied up near the meetinghouse, and Captain and Mrs. Baldwin walked quickly toward the building. From down the street came the Heard family and the Otises. From the river path came the Paines and the fishermen and their families. Nearly all the people of the village gathered to witness the pastor's wedding.

Christine could think of only a few who were missing. Among those was Roger Ackley, who had confessed after a week's confinement and had been convicted a fortnight since of his wife's murder. He now awaited his hanging, but she refused to dwell on that. Thoughts of the grisly crime vanished as Christine waited.

Jane peeked in the church doorway, keeping watch for the right moment. At last everyone else was inside and seated. She and Sarah drew Christine to the doorway. Her two friends took the little girls and hurried to their families' pews.

James Dudley was waiting just inside the door. He offered his arm to Christine, and she slipped her hand through it.

She looked past the pews to the area below the pulpit, where Samuel stood with the officiating minister. Samuel looked at her with such love that she could only return his smile and walk toward him.

A rash of doubts tried one last time to assail her. Could she be a good wife? Samuel said she could. A good mother? He insisted she was already. A proper parson's wife? He would teach her.

He reached out and took her hands in his, and she gazed into his eyes. Peace filled her heart.

A Letter To Our Readers

Dear Reader:

In order that we might better contribute to your reading enjoyment, we would appreciate your taking a few minutes to respond to the following questions. We welcome your comments and read each form and letter we receive. When completed, please return to the following:

Fiction Editor
Heartsong Presents
PO Box 719
Uhrichsville, Ohio 44683

1. Did you enjoy reading *Abiding Peace* by Susan Page Davis?
   ❑ Very much! I would like to see more books by this author!
   ❑ Moderately. I would have enjoyed it more if

   _____

   _____

   _____

2. Are you a member of **Heartsong Presents**? ❑ Yes ❑ No
   If no, where did you purchase this book? _____

   _____

3. How would you rate, on a scale from 1 (poor) to 5 (superior), the cover design? _____

4. On a scale from 1 (poor) to 10 (superior), please rate the following elements.

   ____ Heroine   ____ Plot
   ____ Hero   ____ Inspirational theme
   ____ Setting   ____ Secondary characters

5. These characters were special because? _____

_____

_____

6. How has this book inspired your life? _____

_____

_____

7. What settings would you like to see covered in future
   Heartsong Presents books? _____

_____

_____

8. What are some inspirational themes you would like to see
   treated in future books? _____

_____

_____

9. Would you be interested in reading other **Heartsong
   Presents** titles? ❏ Yes ❏ No

10. Please check your age range:
    ❏ Under 18   ❏ 18-24
    ❏ 25-34   ❏ 35-45
    ❏ 46-55   ❏ Over 55

Name _____

Occupation _____

Address _____

City, State, Zip_____

MISSOURI
Brides

3 stories in 1

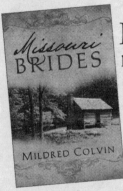

Hope is renewed in three historical romances by Mildred Colvin. Missouri of the early 1800s is full of exciting growth, but for three women, it is filled with lost hopes.

Historical, paperback, 368 pages, 5³/₁₆" x 8"

Heartng

HISTORICAL ROMANCE IS CHEAPER BY THE DOZEN!

Any 12 Heartsong Presents titles for only $27.00*

Buy any assortment of twelve *Heartsong Presents* titles and save 25% off of the already discounted price of $2.97 each!

*plus $4.00 shipping and handling per order and sales tax where applicable. If outside the U.S. please call 740-922-7280 for shipping charges.

HEARTSONG PRESENTS TITLES AVAILABLE NOW:

__HP583	*Ramshackle Rose*, C. M. Hake	__HP656	*Pirate's Prize*, L. N. Dooley
__HP584	*His Brother's Castoff*, L. N. Dooley	__HP659	*Bayou Beginnings*, K. M. Y'Barbo
__HP587	*Lilly's Dream*, P. Darty	__HP660	*Hearts Twice Met*, F. Chrisman
__HP588	*Torey's Prayer*, T. V. Bateman	__HP663	*Journeys*, T. H. Murray
__HP591	*Eliza*, M. Colvin	__HP664	*Chance Adventure*, K. E. Hake
__HP592	*Refining Fire*, C. Cox	__HP667	*Sagebrush Christmas*, B. L. Etchison
__HP599	*Double Deception*, L. Nelson Dooley	__HP668	*Duel Love*, B. Youree
__HP600	*The Restoration*, C. M. Hake	__HP671	*Sooner or Later*, V. McDonough
__HP603	*A Whale of a Marriage*, D. Hunt	__HP672	*Chance of a Lifetime*, K. E. Hake
__HP604	*Irene*, L. Ford	__HP675	*Bayou Secrets*, K. M. Y'Barbo
__HP607	*Protecting Amy*, S. P. Davis	__HP676	*Beside Still Waters*, T. V. Bateman
__HP608	*The Engagement*, K. Comeaux	__HP679	*Rose Kelly*, J. Spaeth
__HP611	*Faithful Traitor*, J. Stengl	__HP680	*Rebecca's Heart*, L. Harris
__HP612	*Michaela's Choice*, L. Harris	__HP683	*A Gentleman's Kiss*, K. Comeaux
__HP615	*Gerda's Lawman*, L. N. Dooley	__HP684	*Copper Sunrise*, C. Cox
__HP616	*The Lady and the Cad*, T. H. Murray	__HP687	*The Ruse*, T. H. Murray
__HP619	*Everlasting Hope*, T. V. Bateman	__HP688	*A Handful of Flowers*, C. M. Hake
__HP620	*Basket of Secrets*, D. Hunt	__HP691	*Bayou Dreams*, K. M. Y'Barbo
__HP623	*A Place Called Home*, J. L. Barton	__HP692	*The Oregon Escort*, S. P. Davis
__HP624	*One Chance in a Million*, C. M. Hake	__HP695	*Into the Deep*, L. Bliss
__HP627	*He Loves Me, He Loves Me Not*, R. Druten	__HP696	*Bridal Veil*, C. M. Hake
		__HP699	*Bittersweet Remembrance*, G. Fields
__HP628	*Silent Heart*, B. Youree	__HP700	*Where the River Flows*, I. Brand
__HP631	*Second Chance*, T. V. Bateman	__HP703	*Moving the Mountain*, Y. Lehman
__HP632	*Road to Forgiveness*, C. Cox	__HP704	*No Buttons or Beaux*, C. M. Hake
__HP635	*Hogtied*, L. A. Coleman	__HP707	*Mariah's Hope*, M. J. Conner
__HP636	*Renegade Husband*, D. Mills	__HP708	*The Prisoner's Wife*, S. P. Davis
__HP639	*Love's Denial*, T. H. Murray	__HP711	*A Gentle Fragrance*, P. Griffin
__HP640	*Taking a Chance*, K. E. Hake	__HP712	*Spoke of Love*, C. M. Hake
__HP643	*Escape to Sanctuary*, M. J. Conner	__HP715	*Vera's Turn for Love*, T. H. Murray
__HP644	*Making Amends*, J. L. Barton	__HP716	*Spinning Out of Control*, V. McDonough
__HP647	*Remember Me*, K. Comeaux		
__HP648	*Last Chance*, C. M. Hake	__HP719	*Weaving a Future*, S. P. Davis
__HP651	*Against the Tide*, R. Druten	__HP720	*Bridge Across the Sea*, P. Griffin
__HP652	*A Love So Tender*, T. V. Batman	__HP723	*Adam's Bride*, L. Harris
__HP655	*The Way Home*, M. Chapman	__HP724	*A Daughter's Quest*, L. N. Dooley
		__HP727	*Wyoming Hoofbeats*, S. P. Davis

(If ordering from this page, please remember to include it with the order form.)

Presents

Great Inspirational Romance at a Great Price!

Heartsong Presents books are inspirational romances in
contemporary and historical settings, designed to give you an
enjoyable, spirit-lifting reading experience. You can choose
wonderfully written titles from some of today's best authors like
Wanda E. Brunstetter, Mary Connealy, Susan Page Davis,
Cathy Marie Hake, Joyce Livingston, and many others.

When ordering quantities less than twelve, above titles are $2.97 each.
Not all titles may be available at time of order.

HEARTSONG
PRESENTS

If you love Christian romance...

$10.⁹⁹

You'll love Heartsong Presents' inspiring and faith-filled romances by today's very best Christian authors...Wanda E. Brunstetter, Mary Connealy, Susan Page Davis, Cathy Marie Hake, and Joyce Livingston, to mention a few!

When you join Heartsong Presents, you'll enjoy four brand-new, mass market, 176-page books—two contemporary and two historical—that will build you up in your faith when you discover God's role in every relationship you read about!

Imagine...four new romances every four weeks—with men and women like you who long to meet the one God has chosen as the love of their lives...all for the low price of $10.99 postpaid.

To join, simply visit www.heartsong presents.com or complete the coupon below and mail it to the address provided.

Mass Market 176 Pages